Misconduct

Misconduct

Beverly Scudamore

James Lorimer & Company Ltd., Publishers
Toronto

James Lorimer & Company Ltd. acknowledges the support of the Ontario Arts Council. We acknowledge the support of the Government of Canada through the Book Publishing Industry Development Program (BPIDP) for our publishing activities. We acknowledge the support of the Canada Council for the Arts for our publishing program. We acknowledge the support of the Government of Ontario through the Ontario Media Development Corporation's Ontario Book Initiative.

Cover illustration: Greg Ruhl

The Canada Council | Le Conseil des Arts
for the Arts | du Canada

ONTARIO ARTS COUNCIL
CONSEIL DES ARTS DE L'ONTARIO

Library and Archives Canada Cataloguing in Publication
Scudamore, Beverly, 1956-
        Misconduct / Beverly Scudamore

(Sports stories; 72)
ISBN-13: 978-1-55028-855-1 (boards)
ISBN-10: 1-55028-855-5 (boards)
ISBN-13: 978-1-55028-854-4 (pbk.)
ISBN-10: 1-55028-854-7 (pbk.)

I. Title. II. Series: Sports stories (Toronto, Ont.); 72.

PS8587.C82M58 2004   jC813.'54   C2004-904821-X

James Lorimer & Co. Ltd,
Publishers
317 Adelaide Street West,
Suite 1002
Toronto, Ontario
M5V 1P9
www.lorimer.ca

Distributed in the United States by:
Orca Book Publishers
P.O. Box 468
Custer, WA USA
98240-0468

Printed and bound in Canada.

CONTENTS

For James

Special thanks to
"Coach" Phil Warner
and his son, Josh, a left winger,
for their assistance with this story.

1 Hockey Camp

"Skate! Dig those blades in! I want to see power!"

The camp instructor paused. His voice darkened. "You'll have to speed up. I-I can't hold the fish back much longer …"

I pushed harder. Not that it mattered — he was going to sic the sturgeon on us anyway. Rounding the end boards, I heard shouting and saw the instructor struggling with Spike, the two hundred pound Junior B mascot. "Agghhh! Down, boy. Your fish breath is killing me."

Someone mimicked the *Jaws* music: "Da-da … da-da … da-da-da-da …"

I braced myself, knowing what was going to happen next. Suddenly Spike broke loose and charged, his fins pumping through the air. Players scattered as the big fish knocked them over, one after another. Considering his size, he gave gentle, yet effective, body checks. The guy in the fish suit was Trent Sowinski, a

Junior B hockey player and an instructor at hockey camp. They were teaching us how to take a hit, fall and get up quickly.

August in Lakeside, Ontario, is a time when most kids head to the beaches to swim or toss Frisbees and footballs. Some simply stretch out on towels and turn into fried zombies.

Then there are the hockey players. Kids like me who bust their butts in a cold arena for a whole month. Each morning we drag ourselves out of bed to make camp on time, and at the end of the day we drag ourselves home dead tired. Why do we do this? It's fun. Also, it's to get in shape for September tryouts.

This year, I, Matthew Gander (a.k.a. Goose), was going to earn a spot playing right wing on the rep hockey team. Last year I was on the A/E (alternate entry) team, and was one of the best players. Now, I was going for the next level. Competition was the only problem. It was going to be tough.

Over two hundred kids had signed up for Pee Wee hockey camp. They filled all three rinks at the Shoreline Arena. Eleven and twelve year olds ranging from house league to Triple A were out to improve their game.

Trent removed his fish head and called the group over. "Nice going. You're getting faster. Three days, and already you're wearing me out." He struggled out of the costume. "Listen up, I want the red and green jerseys to head to the dressing rooms, get changed, and report to the training room for a video on stick-checking. Black and blue teams, get ready to scrimmage."

Muttering, I skated to the bench with Chen Lee and Jason Webster. "I'm still sore from the last time we played the blue team," I told them.

Chen removed his helmet and pushed his sweaty bangs out of his eyes. "Yeah, they smoked us."

Jason grimaced. "It's that new guy."

"Number two," I said. "He played defense against me last time. His name is Dillon McPhail. He's one hard hitter, and he's built like a brick. I hear he played Triple A last year."

I grabbed my water bottle and took a drink. Just then, my line got called to the ice. As I skated to the face-off circle, number two came alongside me, laughing, like he had just heard the world's funniest joke.

I shot him a look. "What's so funny?"

"Your name," he replied. Then he flapped his free arm and went, "Honk! Honk!"

Before I could respond, he skated away.

Trent called, "Hurry up, Goose, we haven't got all day."

I had no choice but to forget about it.

Once the black and blue teams got in position, the linesman dropped the puck. The two centres' sticks clashed and they got into a shoving match, leaving the puck sitting by the red dot. I waited, knees crouched, eyes trained on the puck, ready to respond.

Finally, they worked their sticks free. The black centre directed the puck to me. I picked it up and stickhandled along the boards. Out of the corner of my eye, I spotted Dillon. He was closing in on an angle, charging straight for me. Cutting back, I flipped the puck to my left winger, who sprinted toward the net and shot the puck at the goal. In a split-second, Dillon threw himself onto the ice, blocking the fast wrist shot. The puck bounced off his leg. Lunging forward, I grabbed it and found an opening. I drew my stick back, and was about to shoot, when the puck vanished. Whirling around, I came face to face with Dillon. How had he gotten up so fast? And how had he poke-checked the puck without me knowing?

With a burst of speed, Dillon raced behind the blue net with the puck. He skated end to end, flipping the puck over the goalie's shoulder to score. Insane!

On my next shift, our centre was carrying the puck down the middle when Dillon knocked him off his feet with a solid hip check. On his way down, he managed to sweep the puck sideways. Circling back, I picked it up by the boards. As I advanced into the blue team's zone, Dillon was on me, skating backwards, his eyes fixed on my chest, waiting for my next move.

Keep cool, I told myself. Don't let him psych you out.

All of a sudden, he called, "Honk! Honk!"

I looked up, and he slipped his stick around my ankle, giving a tug. My feet flew into the air and I crashed down hard on my back.

"Fly, birdie, fly!" he laughed.

The ref signalled tripping. As Dillon headed to the penalty box, I met him face to face. "What's your problem?" I roared.

"Chill!" he replied. "I was kidding. It's only camp."

Trent skated over. "What's up?"

Dillon gave an innocent shrug. "We're just talking."

"Yeah, well, talk later," he said. "Ice time is expensive."

During the rest of the scrimmage, Dillon was all over me, delivering hit after hit. After suffering a humiliating 5–1 loss to the blue team, the head instructor announced, "Time for a vitamin D break. Get changed and meet outside on the soccer field for lunch."

Coming out of the arena, the noonday heat felt like being in an oven. The air was thick and hard to breathe. What the weather lady calls a "smog day."

Chen, Jason and I grabbed our boxed lunches from a long table and headed for the shade under a maple tree. There, we crumpled to the ground, exhausted from the morning workout. Four girls came and sat down close by, but they ignored us. They were only interested in the shade.

Curious to see what was for lunch, I flipped the cardboard lid open: a warm burger with a side of nachos and cheese sauce. Mmm... This camp knew how to treat hockey players.

We dove into our meals. I wolfed down half my burger before I came up for air.

"Dillon's been bugging me for two days," I said, sampling the cheese sauce.

"So I've noticed," Jason said, spraying bits of bun into the air.

"I don't get it," I said. "What's his problem?" What I meant was, why me?

It didn't make sense. Rule Number One in bullying is "cool" guys don't get picked on. So what if my hair looks like straw, and I haven't had a growth spurt in a while? Better than some of the guys I've seen around.

"Hey!"

I looked up. Dillon McPhail loomed over me. His baseball cap was turned backwards, and his large ears flopped out under the rim. "Sorry for what happened out there," he said. "If you wanna be called Goose, that's cool with me."

Chen leaned over and snickered. "He wants to be your friend."

I didn't say a word — just crunched hard on a nacho chip, waiting for him to leave. He sat down with his lunch.

"Nice tattoo," he said, examining Jason's thick forearm. "A hound dog with attitude."

"That's Digger," Jason said. "A cartoon character I made up. It's just pen."

"Well, you're good." He looked impressed. "You can draw on my arm any time."

Jason's face lit up. He took his art seriously. By the age of seven, he knew he wanted to be an animator when he grew up. Talk about a sweet career — drawing cartoon characters and making them come to life on a computer.

"So …" Dillon said, digging into his lunch, "have you guys lived here long?"

"Just our whole lives," Jason said.

"Whoa!" Dillon grimaced. "*Lifers?*"

"You make it sound like a jail sentence," Chen commented.

He narrowed his eyes. "That's how it feels."

Jason smothered a chip in cheese sauce and popped the whole thing in his mouth. "Where are you from?" he asked.

"Toronto."

Chen sat up at attention. "Ever go to a Leaf game?"

"A couple times. I sat in the nosebleed section. But, who cares? Tickets are hard to get."

Jason's eyes grew wide. "That's awesome. I'd give anything to go to a game."

"Don't forget Wonderland," Chen said. "Those roller coasters are wicked."

"I had a season's pass," Dillon said, as though it was no big deal. "Their water park rocks."

The Leafs. Wonderland! It was too much. "You are so lucky!" I blurted.

"You think?" His smile widened to reveal a set of clenched teeth. "Look at me now. I'm stuck in this hole."

I sat up on my elbows. "So ... why'd ya move?"

"My parents," he growled. "Dad said he was tired of living in a big city, and Mom insisted she wanted to retire near the lake. That's what they said. But my mom's not even old. And now, Dad has to commute two hours to work. He spends most of the week in Toronto." He paused. "Wanna know the real reason we moved?"

The three of us nodded mutely.

He drilled a finger at his chest. "They didn't like my friends. Mom kept ragging on me about Spider and Luke. Just because they got in a bit of trouble."

This was getting interesting. I leaned forward so I wouldn't miss anything. "Like what?" I inquired.

"Just stuff ... you know, like getting suspended from school and throwing eggs at cars. Nothin' big."

Silence. None of us knew how to respond. Finally, Chen spoke. "Commuting to Toronto must be tough on your dad."

"Not for long," he said. "I'm going to show them. I can create just as much trouble in Lakeside. After I'm through here, my parents will start packing to leave."

Even though I had just met the guy, somehow, I believed him.

2 Hit and Hurt

Throughout the week, I got to know Dillon better, and it seemed I had misjudged him. At hockey camp, he was a lot of fun. He took some crazy chances, just messing around, but doing things that most of us wouldn't dare. Once, he switched the instructional video for a James Bond flick. Another time, he filled my team's water bottles with Powerade — pretty decent of him when he wasn't on our team. I wondered how he got his hands on those drinks. Something told me I didn't want to know.

On the weekend, a bunch of guys from camp met at the school to play ball hockey. As we were setting up the teams, my friend, Kassy Laskaris, walked by.

"Kassy," I called, "Wanna play?"

She started over, then veered away when she noticed Dillon.

"Come back," I called. "We need a goalie."

She kept walking, pretending not to hear me.

Weird. Kassy never refused a chance to play in net.

After dinner, she came banging on my door. "We need to talk." Taking my hand in hers, she added, "It's important."

"Okay." I yanked my hand back. "Come in."

Kassy and I had been friends since nursery school. She could climb any tree, and was a good soccer player.

Kassy followed me into the kitchen. "Want some pop or juice?" I offered.

"No thanks." She flipped her long, dark hair over her shoulders. "I don't have much time, so I'll get straight to the point. It's about Dillon." She sat down at the kitchen table while I poured myself some orange juice.

"What about him?"

"He moved onto my block at the end of June, right after school got out. The neighbours held a street party and ..."

"Party!" I spilt some juice on the floor. "How come I wasn't invited?"

"Come on! You live on Dune Road," Kassy groaned. "Only people who live on Sandhill Street get to go."

I shot her a look. "Why didn't you say it was a street party?"

She scratched her nose. "I did."

"Did not."

"Jerk!" She fired one of her hair elastics at me.

"Anyway, as I'm getting ready for the three-legged race, I notice Dillon standing by the food table. So I yell, 'Hurry! Or you'll miss the kids' races.'"

"He jumps back, looking suspicious. I get the feeling he is up to something. But all he says is, 'Races are stupid.'"

"'Not when there are prizes,' I tell him. Later, when it's time to eat, Mr. Cameron pores himself a glass of punch, and ... you know he can't see." She paused.

"Yeah," I said, "So ...?"

"So-o-o-o ... he's about to take a drink when Amy Porter calls out, 'Mr. Cameron, there's a guppy in your glass!'"

"He didn't ..."

Kassy cracked a grin. "Mr. Cameron can't hear either. So he calls Amy over and says, 'Tell me about this puppy in your class.' Before Amy can stop him, he chugs down the punch."

"Yeah, right!"

"Yep! Then, all of a sudden, he gets a funny look on his face, coughs, and a fish goes flying across the food table. It lands on top of the fancy white cake Sophie's mom brought. The guppy is flopping in the icing, so I run and rescue the poor thing. Well, you know Sophie. She starts screaming about food contamination and fish viruses ..."

The thought of Sophie Sterol flipping out made

me laugh. "Looks good on her," I said. "She deserved it."

"Sophie's not exactly your biggest fan, either," Kassy pointed out. "Not after you tried to infect her with that wart on your thumb."

"What?" I shrugged innocently. "You mean last year ... in line dancing?"

She nodded slowly.

"It wasn't my fault — the teacher made us hold hands."

"That's not the way Sophie tells it. She says you kept jabbing your wart in her face."

"So what! She asked for it — telling the whole class that I had a wart!"

"Whatever." Kassy said, heading to the door. "I can't stick around. I'm going to Amy's for a sleepover." Before she left, she grabbed me, pulling me close. "Watch out for Dillon," she warned. "He's mean."

"Don't worry," I said, pushing her away. "I can handle it."

Most likely, Kassy was right. The guppy incident sounded like Dillon's brand of fun — warped and a bit cruel. Still, it

didn't make him dangerous. At least, that's what I told myself. That was before the illegal hit.

It happened during the second week of camp. That morning Dillon was in a foul mood. I had just pulled on my black jersey, when he entered the dressing room. Dillon didn't want to talk about it, just muttered about getting into a fight with his mom over something to do with hockey. Before long, the washroom door caught the end of his fist.

The black and blue teams began the day with a scrimmage. The puck was in the blue team's end. I had just finished skating past the net and into the corner after a loose puck. When I reached out to nab it, Dillon came up from behind. C-R-UNCH! He slammed me headfirst into the boards. Seeing stars, I crumpled to the ice and lay there stunned.

Checking from behind is one of the dirtiest moves in hockey. It can take a player out of the game for good.

The ref didn't see the hit. As I lay on the ice, counting tiny twinkling lights, he skated over. "Are you all right?" he asked, looking concerned.

Before I could answer, Dillon butted in. "It was a clean hit."

When the stars cleared, I flipped out. "You creamed me from behind! You call that clean?"

Dillon shook his head. "What? You can't take it?"

I called him a few choice names before the ref warned me to cool down.

"Me, cool down!" I shot back. "I'm not the one who —"

"Listen, son," he said, "either control your temper or get off the ice."

When the ref skated away, Dillon grabbed my jersey. "Better toughen up," he snarled. "This is Pee Wee hockey. There's a new set of rules. Hit and hurt."

"Are you kidding?" I said, trying to keep a steady voice. "Do you want to get kicked out?"

He didn't answer. But there was a dangerous look in his eyes.

The head instructor blew the whistle and called everyone over. "For some of you, this is your first year of contact hockey," he began. "At the Pee Wee level we teach you how to give and receive a bodycheck. It takes practice to learn how to do this well. At hockey camp we teach you proper techniques in stages. Since we don't want anyone getting hurt, there will be no bodychecking during scrimmages until the last week."

Dillon hit the boards with his stick. "This sucks! I've been bodychecking for two years."

The instructor responded, "It's a new skill for the house league players. As for the rest of you, it's a good opportunity to review proper technique. Safety comes first here."

Dillon glared at me through his mask. The guy was no friend of mine. My plan was simple. I'd steer clear of him, and in two weeks time hockey camp would be over. Then I'd be rid of him for good. Wait a minute … Kassy said that Dillon lived on Sandhill Street. That was in my neighbourhood! What if he enrolled at my school in September? What if he was in my class?

3 School Daze

Standing alone in left field, my eyes scanned the schoolyard. Lakeside Elementary looked the same as before the summer break. Marco Moscone's soccer ball was still stuck in a tree; the same groups of kids were hanging out together; the yellow graffiti that read Lakeside Rules highlighted the side of the red brick building.

A bunch of us had brought our gloves and convinced the teacher on yard duty to let us fetch a bat and ball from the gym. It beat standing around waiting for the bell, looking as excited as we probably all felt.

"Look out, Goose!"

Glancing up, I saw a pop fly heading for my head. In a split second, I shot my glove up, deflecting the baseball away from my face. Chen came sprinting from the infield, his skinny legs pumping. He scooped up the ball and fired it to second base. "Get in the game!"

he yelled, as he ran back to his position. "We've got to hold up the runner on second base."

The next hitter slammed a ground ball that was scooped up by the shortstop. Yanking my sweaty hand out of my glove, I glanced down at my watch and, for the first time that morning, smiled. It looked like Dillon had enrolled at another school. With any luck, he had enrolled on another planet.

The bell rang. Yes! Punching the air, I jogged off the field. Not only was it the first day of school; more importantly, the first round of tryouts was scheduled for that night. After supper I would head to the Shoreline Arena, impress the coaches, and hopefully earn a spot on the "A" team. Since Dillon played Triple A, I wouldn't have to worry about meeting up with him at the arena. Yep, things were looking up.

Not taking any chances, I turned for one last look. A blue car caught my attention as it pulled into the parking lot. The passenger door opened. Sure enough, Dillon stepped out, slamming the door behind him. I stood without moving as he headed up the sidewalk. He crossed in front of me, moving fast and glaring straight ahead. A fat wad of gum rolled around in his cheek. On his T-shirt was a picture of a snake crawling through the eye of a skull. Lakeside's newest student was dressed to scare.

I ran ahead to alert Chen and Jason. "Look who's here," I said, motioning with my head.

"Man, those are serious spikes!" Jason observed. "They look like nails."

Chen laughed. "Crazy hair gel."

I got straight to the point. "What if he's in our class?"

Jason gave me a reassuring look. "Who cares? He's probably in the split."

"Why'd you say that?" I asked, suddenly hopeful.

Jason punched my arm playfully. "Because it's what you want me to say."

I didn't laugh.

"Don't look now," Chen said, "he's coming this way."

"I'm gone," I blurted. "See you guys inside."

Chen pointed to the mob in front of the door. "Okay,

Houdini. Let's see you magically disappear."

"No problem." Elbowing my way through the jungle of arms and legs, I vanished inside the school.

Mrs. Carson, the Grade 6 teacher stood in the doorway, greeting her new students as they filed into the classroom.

Sophie knocked my arm as she ran past. "Eww," she moaned, tossing her hair. "I could get lice."

Getting stuck with Sophie Sterol in my class was more bad luck. She had major issues, mostly about germs and guys. She treated boys like fungus. And after the wart incident in Grade 5, I was number one on her parasite list.

I waited in the hall for Jason and Chen to make sure we sat together. By the time they arrived, most of the desks were taken. Chen pointed down the second aisle. "Three in a row!"

We took off at a run. Jason and Chen slid into the first two empty desks. As I was about to claim the third, Sophie stood up, blocking my way.

"Get lost, Matthew!" she ordered, jabbing a polished fingernail at me. "This is Amy Porter's desk."

"You're not allowed to save desks," I informed her.

She stared at me with her fish eyes — round and unblinking disks. "Amy's school supplies are already in the desk. Mrs. Carson sent her to the office to deliver a note."

Reaching into the desk, I brought out a pen and shoved it in her hand. "You call this school supplies?"

She curled her upper lip at me. "Grow up!"

"Make me," I challenged.

"Okay, you asked for it!" Directing her voice at the teacher, she yelled, "Matt Gander pushed me!"

"Wh-what are you talking about?" I backed away from the desk. "I didn't touch you!"

Mrs. Carson turned from the blackboard, and glared. "Matthew, find an empty desk and sit down."

I was about to leave, when Sophie opened her mouth. "Too bad, you lose."

"Because you lie!" I shot back

"And you've got warts!"

"Shut up!"

Mrs. Carson marched over, shaking a finger at me. "There will be no such language in this class. The new principal is very busy this morning, but I am sure he could make time for you."

"Sorry," I mumbled, avoiding her eyes. I couldn't look up. If I did, she would see that I was not sorry at all.

Mrs. Carson stood, hands on hips, waiting. Finally, she dropped the bomb on me. "You owe Sophie an apology."

A hush fell over the class and everyone watched with interest. "B-but!"

"Go ahead!" Mrs. Carson demanded, tapping her shoe.

No fair! I was the victim. First, I was wrongly accused. Then, I had to suffer the humiliation of having my wart problem exposed for the second time. And now this! Crossing my fingers, I muttered, "Sorry."

By the time Mrs. Carson had finished with me, the rest of the class was seated. I looked up and down the aisles until my eyes came to rest upon the last empty desk — at the far side by the windows.

Oh, man! How could one kid have such bad luck? He must have walked in while I was under attack.

Kassy gave me a friendly wave as I headed over. Dillon blew a bubble and grinned. He raised his hand for a high-five, acting like we were old buddies. Did the guy have a short memory?

When I sat down, he turned around in his desk. "What's with that girl? She's got a big mouth."

"Yeah, I know," I muttered.

Mrs. Carson sat at her desk reading the reply Amy had brought from the office. Somehow she still managed to hear someone chewing gum, and zero in on the guilty mouth.

"Gum is not allowed in the classroom," she explained calmly, pointing to the garbage pail.

Sucking in his cheeks, Dillon fired the wad halfway across the room. Bull's-eye! Straight into the can.

I sat back, waiting for Mrs. Carson to dole out a nasty punishment. Weird! She didn't say a word. She just kept reading. It didn't make sense. She had just threatened to sic the principal on me. Guess she was giving him a break because he was new.

A few minutes later, Mrs. Carson stood and gave the class a friendly smile.

"Welcome to a brand new year at Lakeside Elementary," she began. "As I look around the room, I see a lot of familiar faces. And I am pleased to announce that our school has a new student. His name is Dillon McPhail. Please stand, Dillon, so everyone can meet you."

He didn't budge.

Mrs. Carson's smile shrunk. "Everyone, please welcome Dillon."

"Hi, Dillon," the class chorused.

He stared down at his desk.

Mrs. Carson's lips tightened. She must have sensed this year was going to be tough.

4 Tryout Trauma

At home, I hurled my backpack up the stairs. "He shoots!" Upon hearing a thud outside my bedroom door, I punched the air: "He scores!"

From upstairs came the sound of Mom "welcoming" me home. "Matthew, get up here this instant! I could have broken my neck falling over your backpack."

"Coming, Mom." Bolting up the stairs, I kicked my backpack through the doorway. Mom met up with me in the hallway and asked all the usual questions about the first day of school.

Julie, my five-year-old sister, ran out of her bedroom, holding a glitter pony in each hand. Her hair was tangled in coloured elastics.

"I made pigtails," she announced, tipping her head from side to side. "All by myself!"

"Good for you," I said, with a bored nod.

"Wanna play? You can be the unicorn."

"Not now," I said, "I've got tryouts tonight." Escaping to my bedroom, I closed the door and put on a CD.

At supper, Julie was busy playing with her hair while Mom and Dad talked about work. Dad manages a department store and Mom is a pharmacy assistant. They work in the same mall, but rarely on the same shift. That way they don't have to fork out a pile of money on babysitters. This means we don't all eat together much.

I smothered my chicken in ketchup and was about to start chowing down when Mom turned to me. "By the way, Matt, I've been meaning to tell you something."

She sounded serious, so I put down my fork and listened. I was still trying to get used to her carrot-orange hair — a big change from the old brown.

"Mrs. Laskaris introduced me to her new neighbour at the grocery store," she began. "Her name is Donna McPhail, and she has a son in Grade 6 at Lakeside." She paused, expecting me to add something.

"His name is Dillon," I offered. "I met him at hockey camp."

"Oh, good," Mom said, smiling. "Mrs. McPhail told me that Dillon is having a hard time making new friends. Moving can be difficult."

I set my jaw and glared. Mom noticed my reaction,

but pressed on. "When Mrs. McPhail told me that Dillon is going to be at the tryouts tonight, I ..."

"No!" I stabbed the chicken with my fork. Ketchup sprayed across the table. "No, no, *no*!"

Mom sat back, stiff in her chair. "Mrs. McPhail offered to drive you to the arena. I have to work tonight, and Dad's staying home with Julie. She is exhausted after her first full day of senior kindergarten."

"Forget it!" I snapped. "I'd rather walk."

Mom clicked her tongue. "Matthew, what's the matter?"

I didn't answer.

Dad stroked his moustache thoughtfully. "Being the new kid in town isn't easy, son. Would it hurt you to act friendly?"

"Yeah, but Dad —"

Mom spoke up before I could finish. "Honestly," she said, shaking her head, "it's just a car ride. We have to help each other in this family."

Suddenly Julie screamed. "Matt got ketchup on my pony!" Tears rolled down her cheeks. Without a word, Mom grabbed the pony and took it to the sink.

"Fine," I surrendered. "When do I leave?"

"Mrs. McPhail will pick you up in twenty minutes," Mom said, her voice brightening.

Dad reached out and patted me on the back. "I'll even do the dishes for you tonight."

I shoved my plate aside and left the table without

dessert. Gathering up my equipment, I waited on the front porch until the McPhail's car pulled into our driveway. After I stashed my bag in the trunk, I slid into the backseat with my stick.

"Nice to meet you, Matt," Mrs. McPhail said, greeting me with a warm smile. She seemed way too normal to have a mess-up for a son.

Dillon ignored me, staring out the window.

"Why aren't you trying out for Triple A?" I said.

"My parents won't let me," he mumbled.

Whoa! Talk about surprise.

Mrs. McPhail stopped at a red light and turned to face me. "Dillon's father is out of town a lot," she explained. "The travel commitment at the Triple A level is more than I can handle alone."

Dillon looked at me, tight-lipped. "My dad's an investment manager. He takes care of *other* people."

Maybe that's why Dillon had been fighting with his mom that day at hockey camp. Being told he couldn't try out for Triple A hockey must have sucked. Still, that didn't make it okay to plow me headfirst into the boards. Dillon stared out the window, and I did the same.

When the car pulled into the Shoreline Arena parking lot, we grabbed our stuff from the trunk and walked off to separate dressing rooms.

★ ★ ★

Once I got dressed, I stood at the gate with the other players while the Zamboni flooded the ice.

"Good luck," Jason said, slapping my helmet. "Hope you fall on your face."

"Watch out," I replied. "I'm planning to beat you."

"Yeah, sure," he said, grinning.

I gave an awkward laugh. It felt weird, both of us trying out for the same position. Chances are only one of us would make it.

Chen came up behind us. "Bad news," he said. "Fifty-four kids are trying out for the team. The coach had to divide tonight's tryout into two shifts."

My head dropped. "Brutal."

"The team is allowed seventeen players," he went on. "That means the coach will be making thirty-seven cuts." He ran his glove across his throat.

That's all I needed to hear. My confidence took a dip in the toilet. I mean, who was I kidding? I'd have to play like a superstar.

"What's the coach looking for?" I asked.

"How should I know?" Chen said.

"You played 'A' last year."

"Yeah, but it was a different coach. Just act like you really want it. And no matter what, never give up."

The Zamboni made its final lap, before rumbling off the ice. Chen began skating slowly, reaching his hands to his toes. "Better get good and loose," he said. "This is going to be one tough workout."

Slow wasn't working for me. I needed to burn off a ton of nervous energy, so I started to skate hard. As I rounded the first corner, a stick jabbed at my tailbone. "Honk! Honk!"

I was already on edge, so it didn't take much for me to blow. "Back off!" I yelled, swinging my stick.

"Keep your stick on the ice," Dillon warned, skating alongside me. "The coaches are watching."

Sure enough, I spotted a group of men holding clipboards.

Dillon took off, weaving through the players, making the rest of us look like we were attending the family skate.

The whistle blew, and someone directed us to the far end of the rink where we sat down on the ice. A man with grey hair, wearing an autographed ball cap, stepped onto the ice. He was dressed in shorts and running shoes, and he walked with a limp.

"Yes!" I perked up, instantly recognizing him.

"Hi, guys," he said, tipping his cap. "My name is Skip Fraser. I have the privilege of coaching minor Pee Wee hockey this season."

For as long as I could remember, Skip had been coaching minor hockey at the Shoreline Arena. According to my dad, he had been a local hero years ago, playing Junior B with the Lakeside Wave, then a university hockey team. NHL teams were scouting him when he got injured.

"I'm going to watch you scrimmage today," he told us. "I'll be looking at your skating, how well you handle the puck and your shooting. But I also want to see teamwork. I don't care how skilled you are — if you can't remember that hockey is a team sport, you won't make this team. Above all, I want to see effort. Show me that you want to play."

"Are you making cuts?" Marco asked, his voice cracking.

"Relax," Skip said. "No final decisions will be made tonight."

He divided us into two squads. Dillon, Marco and I slipped on white pinnie scrimmage vests. Chen and Jason wore red. For once, I didn't have to play against Dillon. Hockey would be a safer game — for me, at least.

A line from each squad skated to centre ice and got in position for the face-off. I stood ready on right wing, nervously gripping my stick. A man standing by the gate grabbed a puck and skated onto the ice.

"Hey, guys," he said, waving a gloved hand. "My name is Ray Scott, your assistant coach. We are going to play one-minute shifts, changing on the fly at the sound of the buzzer. You've got sixty seconds to show me what you can do. Go for it. Play hard, but fair."

Mr. Scott dropped the puck. Marco kicked it into the open with his skate.

Now's my chance! I darted after the loose puck.

Out of the corner of my eye, I saw a red pinnie closing in fast. Determined to get to the puck first, I reached out with my stick. The guy brushed past, barely nudging me. I lost an edge and fell over like a limp leaf. What?

Calm down, I told myself. No white envelopes are being handed out tonight.

Before I could do anything, the buzzer sounded. As I skated to the bench, I glanced over at Skip, who was scribbling comments in the clipboard.

"Nice try," a winger named Kyle said, as I took my place on the bench.

"You tanked out there!" Dillon called from the opposite end.

The player standing next to me on the bench nudged me, "Hey, I've got a good one."

I turned. "What?"

"Why don't ghosts make good goalies?"

I wasn't in the mood for jokes, but I went along. "Why?"

"The pucks go right through them."

The joke was dumb, but I laughed.

At the buzzer, Dillon launched himself full speed from the bench. The guy was a missile; he was locked on target. Once he got his stick on the puck, it was his alone. He sped down the ice, deking out the opposition. Closing in on the net, he wound up, and slammed the puck between the goalie's legs to score. He made everyone on that shift look bad, especially the goalie, who hadn't even seen the puck coming.

When Dillon left the ice, Skip patted him on the back. "Nice, number two, but you're not going to make the team that way. On your next shift, show me that you can pass the puck."

Dillon grabbed a water bottle and walked up to me. "What's with the coach? I was the reason my team won their division last year. Playing defence, I still scored thirty-two goals — most of them unassisted. At the end of the year, I got MVP."

I shrugged. "Skip believes in team play."

"Yeah, well, I believe in winning," he muttered, returning to his spot on the bench.

On my next shift, I managed to stay on my feet and make a clean pass to Marco. Before I could do more, the buzzer rang. When it was all over, I dragged myself off the ice. If I were going to make the team, I'd have to play better next time.

Thursday night was the first round of cuts. That was in two days. After an intense tryout, Skip would hand out sealed white envelopes. He would instruct us to not open them until we got home. Not making the team was bad enough, but bawling like a baby in front of the guys was worse.

After practice, Mrs. McPhail stopped at a variety store to buy Dillon and me cherry slushies. Sitting on the curb, we slurped them back, while Mrs. McPhail went to the gas station. I stared into space, minding my own business.

"What's with the attitude?" Dillon said. "You're not still mad about that hit, are you? It was a freakin' month ago."

"And if I am?" I said flatly.

He put his drink down and studied my face. "What? You want me to say sorry?"

"Like you would anyways," I muttered.

"Okay, I'm sorry."

It was a long time ago. I sat there wondering if I did overreact. After all, things happen when a game heats up. Suddenly my memory kicked in. No!

I took a long, icy slurp through the straw. A knife tore through my brain. I clutched my head. "Aaghhhh! Brain freeze!"

"What a numbskull!" Dillon said. "Get it? Numb skull."

I looked up, and we both laughed. Then he threw me a curve ball. "I was thinking," he said, staring into the cup. "Maybe we could hang out at recess tomorrow."

I opened my mouth to protest, but what could I say?

5 Street Rules

Mrs. Carson stood before the class, clutching a sheet of paper. "This morning we are going to review English terms," she announced. "Who can define 'thesaurus' and explain its use in the classroom?"

Boring.

Mrs. Carson waited patiently. Nobody raised their hand. Students cringed in their desks as her eyes passed over them. Eventually her gaze settled upon Jason.

He smiled, looking strangely confident. "The saurus is the scientific name for a dinosaur family which includes Allosaurus, Stegosaurus and the fierce Tyrannosaurus Rex …" He went on, giving wild facts and describing their strange reptilian shapes. He should know — he spent hours in his bedroom sketching dinosaurs. "But," he concluded, "the saurus is not much use in the classroom, because it is extinct."

The class howled.

"Quiet," Mrs. Carson ordered.

Jason leaned forward in his desk. "I didn't make it up. I can show you my book."

Mrs. Carson didn't know what to make of Jason, so she looked at me instead. "Matthew, define 'thesaurus'."

"Umm … it's a book thing-a-ma-jig … that can make you write better because, like, it helps you change lame words for better ones."

Mrs. Carson nodded slowly. "Thank you, Matthew. I think the thesaurus is going to be useful in this class."

Jason pumped his hand in the air. "Hey, I knew that! I didn't hear right!"

"Okay, okay, let's move on." Turning to Amy, Mrs. Carson said, "Define 'interjection'."

Amy surveyed the class for help. Since there were no offers, she did what any good student would do — she took a wild guess. "A needle?"

Mrs. Carson sighed. "That would be an injection."

A couple of kids snickered.

Mrs. Carson placed the paper on her desk. "Obviously, we have a class of comedians today. Well, I am going to hand out the list of twenty English terms for you to complete alone at your desks. Write a definition for each term — and *please* use a proper reference book. What you do not finish in class is homework."

Mrs. Carson was tough. The real lesson of the day: it didn't pay to play in her class.

When the sheets were passed out, I got straight to work. No way was I doing homework that night. Part way down the list, someone whacked me on the forehead. An eraser bounced off my head and onto the floor. I looked up at Dillon.

"So … are we hanging out at recess?"

Fortunately, I had come to school armed with a reply. "I'm playing soccer at recess."

"Okay," he said. "I'll play, too."

Geez, was there no escaping this guy? I returned to the page.

★ ★ ★

After school, the sun was still blazing hot. Under my baggy pants and long-sleeved shirt my body felt like a furnace. Some kids were heading to the beach, but I had other plans. Jason, Marco and I were meeting at Chen's house with our in-line skates to play ball hockey. Skip scheduled the first round of cuts for the next day, and I needed all the practice I could get.

The pavement on the cul-de-sac was smooth, perfect for blading. At the end of August, I had rotated my wheels, so I was in good shape. Before the scrimmage, we removed pebbles and bits of junk from the road. We didn't want anything to interfere with the game.

I glided over to Chen. "Where's Jayce?"

"At art class," he said, adjusting his elbow pads.

"What?" I shook my head in disbelief. "I thought

he would be here with us? Does he think he's just going to be handed a spot on the rep team?"

Chen shrugged. "He didn't want to miss cartoon drawing."

"Now the teams are uneven," I grumbled.

"Maybe not," Chen said, pointing over his shoulder.

I turned and saw Dillon approaching on in-line skates. He was wearing shorts and a T-shirt. "Who invited him?"

As if to answer my question, Marco called out, "Right on time! You can play on my side. We're a man short."

Playing opposite Dillon without a ref was suicidal. But, hey, I needed the practice, so I stuck around.

We were going three on three — Me, Chen, and his pint-sized neighbour against Marco, Dillon and some guy from another school. There were no goalies, and we were playing street rules — every man for himself.

"Game's on!" Marco called, tossing a tennis ball.

Dillon moved in fast from the opposite side, but I reached the bouncing ball first. Making a tight cut to avoid him, I smacked the ball to Chen. But his neighbour nabbed it, spun around 90 degrees and sent the ball hurtling toward the open net. Dillon scrambled after it, but couldn't catch up. The guy scored.

A few plays later, I started to sweat. Protective equipment is the law in my house. Mom sees a lot of "road rash" at the pharmacy. Also, I busted my arm in Grade 5 playing street hockey. Wearing everything at the arena is a no-brainer because, like, everyone else does the same, but on the streets, unsupervised, and scared of looking uncool ... the right choice is not always easy. I forgot my helmet that day. Chen, on the other hand, wore full gear and didn't care what others thought.

Leaning on my stick, and panting hard, I waited for something to happen. Glancing over at Dillon, I noticed his teeth clenched. When the ball got dropped, he lunged after it, nabbing it in mid-air and knocking it down. It bounced at an odd angle, over to the little kid, who circled back and dropped it off to me. I roared in on the net, pivoting on one heel to deke out Marco. Dillon chugged after me like a transport truck. I dropped my shoulder, made a sharp turn, and flipped the puck to Chen. He closed in on the net and raised his stick. He was about to shoot when Marco reached out with his glove and caught the blade of Chen's stick.

"*Moron!*" Chen called, whirling around, almost knocking Marco off his feet.

Without refs, we had to find our own ways of keeping each other in check.

By this time, the other side was desperate to even-up the score. We held them off until Kassy and Amy walked by.

"How's it going?" Kassy called.

I looked up for a split second and waved. That's all it took for Dillon to rush past me and tie the game at 1–1.

We regrouped and Chen dropped the ball. I went burning after it, right up to the curb. In the race, Marco and I almost collided. Both of us veered at the last second. Wham! I slammed into someone. The impact sent me hurtling onto the pavement. My elbows pads absorbed the hit, as I thrust my arms out to protect my head.

"Whoa, that was nasty!" I said, getting up slowly.

No one said a word. They all stared behind me. Turning, I saw Dillon lying on the ground.

6 Out for Blood

Dillon had landed in a gravel patch at the side of the cul-de-sac. Blood trickled from his elbows and a gash on his left leg.

"Stay here," Chen said, leaning over him. "I'll get my mom." He ran to his house.

Tears streamed down Dillon's face. He looked at me, furious.

"I'm sorry. It was an accident," I tried to explain. "I didn't mean to …"

Mrs. Lee came running down the street in her workclothes. Chen followed close behind, carrying a white first-aid kit. She knelt beside Dillon, carefully inspecting the wounds. "There is a lot of gravel under the skin," she said. "I think you should see a doctor. Are your parents home?"

Dillon nodded. "My mom is."

Mrs. Lee sent Chen to make the call.

Meanwhile, Dillon glowered at me. "If I can't make

tryouts tomorrow, you are … Ow!" His face twisted in pain.

"Sorry," Mrs. Lee said. She was wrapping gauze around his elbow. "There is an old saying," she said, locking eyes with him. "If you are patient in one moment of anger, you will avoid a hundred days of sorrow."

Dillon looked away.

Mrs. Lee placed a square bandage over the gash on his leg. "Hold this," she instructed him. "Press just enough to stop the bleeding. That's all we can do for now."

A few minutes later Dillon's mom arrived. Her forehead was creased with worry. She tried to help Dillon up, but he pushed her away. "Leave me alone! I can walk by myself."

Mrs. McPhail exchanged an awkward smile with Mrs. Lee. "Thanks for all your help," she said, before hurrying to the car.

"Hey, Goose!" Dillon called from the back window. He made a fist and pounded it in his hand.

I wandered home in a daze. After dinner, I went straight to my room. Dillon McPhail was out to get me.

★ ★ ★

As I lay in bed, images of Dillon threatening, shoving, and pushing rolled through my head. I tossed and turned, sleepless. The thing is, I had never been in a fistfight. Whenever we've had problems, my friends and I just talk or yell or walk away. This was new to me. I considered talking to my parents, but I was afraid they would phone Mrs. McPhail. That would only make things worse.

But hey, I did know a few things about survival: for instance, I knew to keep my arms up to protect my head, and to keep my feet moving so I wouldn't make an easy target — and if all failed ... to run — FAST!

After a fitful night, I finally dozed off. Before long, my alarm clock started beeping. I couldn't believe it was already 7:15 in the morning. Lifting my head off the pillow, I reached out and pushed the button. After all, there was no reason to get up.

Sometime later, Mom came bursting into my room. "Matt! It's 8:30. You're going to be late for school!"

Burying my head in the pillow, I moaned. "Oh-h-h ... I don't feel well."

Mom sat on the edge of my bed, staring down at me. "Have you got a fever?" she asked. "Headache? Muscle aches?" Despite all her grilling, I was determined not to crack. Too much was at stake. Holding my stomach, I thrashed about, kicking my bedspread to the floor. A few days of the stomach flu would give Dillon a chance to cool down.

Mom held up the thermometer. "What a shame,"

she said, patting my shoulder. "Getting sick in the middle of tryouts."

Oh, man, I forgot about the tryouts. Some quick thinking was in order. Luckily, I am gifted in the art of timed-air-release. Clutching my stomach, I lurched back and forth, pumping the gases from deep within.

Mom stood up alarmed. "Run! You can make the bathroom!"

I raised a hand to calm her. "Wait, I feel something." After a little more rocking, I released a deep belch. "Ah-h-h!" I sighed with relief. "Much better."

Mom eyed me with suspicion. "Matthew ... what is this all about? Is it the pressure of tryouts? I don't want you to get so wound up, that you make yourself sick. Hockey is supposed to be fun."

"Can't talk now," I said, on the run. "I'm late for school." Grabbing jeans and a T-shirt from the ever-growing pile on the floor, I hurried to the bathroom where I ran my toothbrush across my teeth. Next the blue hair gel. One dab, then a quick finger fix. Presto! No more bed-head and no need for a comb.

Racing down the stairs, I stopped to look out the living room window. Chen and Jason were waiting up the street by the mailbox. There was no time for breakfast. Grabbing a banana from the kitchen table, I put on my backpack, and ran out the door.

Everything will be okay, I told myself. I can count on Jayce and Chen. They will defend me.

Unfortunately, Chen probably wouldn't be much help. He's a good friend, but a lot smaller than the rest of us. Dillon could crush him with his thumb. Jason was my man. He was built like a linebacker.

"Jayce!" I called, running up. "Dillon's after me. You've got to help!"

"Uh ... I don't fight," he pointed out.

"Neither do I!" I fired back. "He's waiting to pounce on me, though. What am I going to do?"

"Think of a better way," he said.

We walked in silence while I mashed my banana in my fist.

A block later, Chen piped up. "Why don't you report him to the office? The principal will stop him."

I kicked a stone off the sidewalk. "Me ... rat on Dillon? Don't you get it? That would make things worse. I have to take care of this."

"But the school has ways of dealing with these things," Chen insisted. "They know how to ..."

Jason cut him off. "Talk to Dillon," he said. "Explain that it was an accident. Get him to back off."

"I already tried that," I said in exasperation. "I told him that yesterday."

"And if that doesn't work," Chen said, "promise to do his homework for a month, for a year — whatever it takes."

I glared at him "You're kidding ... right?"

"Tell you what," Jason said, finally. "When we get

to school, I'll talk to Dillon — you know, find out what he's thinking. Maybe you're getting worked up over nothing."

I didn't have a lot of options. Who knows? Maybe Jayce could convince Dillon to back off. "Okay," I said. "It's worth a try."

Approaching the school, we found Dillon standing by the water fountain talking to some girls from our class.

"Go!" I said, shoving Jayce toward him. "Hurry, before the bell rings."

Jason walked right up to Dillon. Chen and I stayed back, out of sight, around the corner of the building.

7 Fight or Flight

When the bell rang, Jason and Dillon walked to class together. I decided to wait for Jason by the lockers. While I was putting away my backpack, Dillon came up to me. He pulled me to my desk. "Come here. I'll show you something."

I was afraid he wanted to show me his fist. "Dillon, I didn't mean to …"

He propped his leg up on my desk. A large white dressing covered the gash. "Last night, at the hospital, the doctor stuck a needle into my leg to freeze it, but I could still feel her rooting around under my skin with tweezers. She pulled out bits of sand and gravel. I watched the whole thing. After cleaning the cut, she stapled my skin together." As proof, he pulled back part of the bandage to reveal ten metal staples.

"How are your elbows," I inquired cautiously, "are they okay?"

"A few scrapes and bruises."

I sat back confused. Dillon didn't seem angry. He was excited about his trip to the hospital — especially the gory details. Jason must have been convincing.

Now for the big question. "Can you make tryouts tonight?"

"Yep."

"You mean the doctor said okay?"

"Not exactly," he admitted. "After she examined me, she took me to the treatment room. When Mom tried to follow, I asked if I could go alone, explaining that I'm not a little kid anymore. Just as the doctor was finishing up, she got called away on an emergency. Mom didn't get a chance to speak with her."

He paused, grinning.

"Go on," I insisted.

"The nurse met with Mom and gave her a wound-care sheet. Meanwhile, I was trying to drag her out of there, insisting I would fill her in on the details later, including the fact that I could still play hockey."

"No way. Really?"

He nodded. "I wouldn't let a little cut screw up an entire season. Anyway, the staples are on the side of my leg. I'll be fine."

I hesitated. "So ... we're good?"

"Yeah," he said. "Anyway, I realized something last night — we're even now."

"We are?"

"Sure. Remember that day at hockey camp? I hit you bad, but you sure got me back yesterday."

"Wait … it was an accident."

He twirled a finger in the air. "Whatever."

"So … there's a big difference."

"Anyway… I don't go around beating up my friends."

Friends? Coming from Dillon's mouth, that word had an odd sound. But, hey, why should I care if it meant the fight was off?

"But in this case," he said. "I must make an exception."

I sucked air. "What?"

"You can thank your buddy, Jason. Before school he walked up to me demanding to know if I was planning to fight you. Some girls were hanging around listening. I couldn't look like a wimp."

"Trust me," I said, quickly. "No one thinks you're a wimp."

He smiled appreciatively. "Here's how we can settle this. At recess we'll head to the woods where there are no teachers. I'll give you one lame punch. You'll fall to the ground, moaning and crying like a baby, and it'll be over. Everyone will go away happy."

"Not everyone," I pointed out.

A hand slipped on my shoulder, pulling me backwards. "Jason told me what happened," Kassy said. "He says you're scared. Maybe I can help."

I whirled around in my desk. "Jason said *what*?"

She gave me a sympathetic smile. "Just that you're afraid of being beaten up."

What was Jason thinking? That was private stuff between us guys. "Me?" I said, hardening my face. "Afraid? I don't think so. In fact, the fight was my idea."

Her jaw dropped. "Your idea? Are you nuts? Fighting is an automatic suspension. And besides, it's stupid."

Sophie walked past my desk. "Don't bleed on school property," she advised. "You could spread disease."

Marco offered another helpful suggestion. "Transfer to a different school. Today."

By the time Mrs. Carson walked into the room, the entire class was aware of the upcoming fight, and they all planned to attend. To make matters worse, word was out that I was chicken, so I couldn't back down. My pride had taken a major hit.

During the morning I tossed some ideas around in my head. Should I go along with Dillon — take the lame punch and get laughed out of Grade 6, or should I stand up to him and get creamed? Either way, I'd be the loser. How had things gotten so out of control?

At the bell, Dillon stood and motioned for me to follow. The rest of the class got in line behind us. By this point, I was desperate. I needed a way out! As we approached the principal's office, I attempted to duck in, explaining to Dillon. "I just remembered. Mr. LaFond wants to see me."

The crowd pushed me beyond the door. There was no escape. My legs felt like dough. My hands couldn't form a fist. Fear was dissolving my muscles into flab.

We walked to the far end of the schoolyard. Only rarely did a yard-duty teacher wander into the wooded area. The trees were widely spaced, their canopy allowing enough light for bushes and shrubs to grow underneath. Dillon had chosen the perfect cover.

Forming a circle around the two of us, my fellow classmates chanted, "Fight! Fight! Fight!"

In desperation, I searched the crowd for Chen and Jason. They were nowhere in sight. The group closed in like a pack of vultures, sniffing soon-to-be dead meat. "Fight! Fight! Fight!"

Dillon stepped up to me. "This won't hurt … much," he added. He blew on his fist. "For luck," he explained.

Just then, something weird happened. I felt as though I had been plugged into a high voltage power source. A rush of adrenaline pumped raw anger through my veins. Forget the plan — I was not going down that easy!

My jaw set. My hands curled into fists. Dillon saw the change in my eyes. In response, he flexed his arm, revealing a firm muscle. My only hope was to land the first punch.

I drew back my arm, was set to follow through,

when Sophie's voice pierced the air. "Help! Kassy's fainted. Someone get a teacher! Quick!"

My hands dropped. Upon hearing the word "teacher," the crowd scattered. I started to follow, but Dillon pulled me back. He grabbed my shirt, lifting me off the ground.

"Watch it!" I struggled to break free. "You're ripping my shirt!"

"Is that all you've got?" he taunted.

"You asked for it!" I started swinging, landing a solid hit on his shoulder.

Dillon let go of my shirt. He put his hands in the air, like he was surrendering, but he was laughing. "What's your problem? This isn't a real fight."

"What is it then?" I shouted, half-crazed.

"A few guys stayed behind. I couldn't just slink away, like it meant nothin'. Anyway, it's over now — a teacher's coming."

My fists unfolded. It really was over.

We headed out of the woods. "No offence," Dillon said, "but it's obvious you've never been in a fight before."

I didn't argue.

"One thing you should know," he said. "Never punch someone bigger than you in the shoulder. Instead of hurting, it's just going to make him angrier. Then he's going to come after you even harder."

"Now you tell me," I mumbled.

He looked around. "Where are your buddies?"

"Beats me," I said, kicking a tree trunk.

After recess, I was surprised to find Kassy sitting at her desk, chatting happily with Amy. "Why are you here? I thought you were sick."

She tossed her hair behind her shoulders and grinned. "I was *faking*, silly! Brilliant, if you ask me. By attracting a teacher, I prevented the fight without getting you in trouble."

Kassy had saved my butt. I should have been grateful, but instead I snapped at her. "I didn't need your help! It was between Dillon and me."

"I had to stop the fight," she explained. "I didn't want anything to happen to you. After all, I didn't want you to get hurt."

What? Kassy was *worried*?

🎱 A Desperate Move

"Where do dead hockey players skate in winter?"

I tossed my hockey bag on the dressing room floor. "I give up."

"Lake Eerie."

Tonight was the second tryout. I had just been introduced to Craig, Belch, and Nitro — three guys who had played on the "A" team last year. Craig was the one with the jokes. Like me, he was trying out for a position on right wing. Unlike me, he was a shoe-in for a spot.

Belch (otherwise known as Jamie Hamilton) was trying out for defence. The guy talked in burps. He answered questions with blasts of air. A short, squeaky burp indicated "yes." A long, low one meant "no."

Justin Bolt played centre with such explosive force he had earned the name "Nitro."

I was pulling on my practice jersey, when Chen and Jason walked in the dressing room.

Jason waved his smelly shin pad in my face. "I don't get it," he said. "You walked off to fight Dillon. Then, at the next recess, you ditched us to hang out with him. What did we miss?"

"The whole thing," I replied stone-faced.

"Why are you mad?" Chen asked.

"For one thing," I started, as I leaned forward to tie my skates "You didn't even have the guts to watch me go down."

"It's not like that," Chen replied. "The kindergarten teacher grabbed us on the way out. She made us look for a little kid's jacket in the primary yard. We wanted to help."

"Yeah, sure." I let go of my laces and drilled a finger at Jason. "Thanks a lot. You forced Dillon to call a fight."

"What?" He took a step back.

"Then you told Kassy I was scared! That was between us."

"But she's your friend too," Jason said. "And she overheard Dillon say he wanted to fight."

The door swung open and Dillon burst through. I waved him over. It was nice to have a *friend* in the dressing room. He tossed his equipment next to mine. "Ready to kick butt?"

"Yeah, I can't wait."

Chen and Jason grabbed their bags and retreated to the other bench.

A few minutes later, we filed down the

rubber-tiled hallway to the rink. Before we skated onto the ice, Dillon took me aside. "Skip wants to see teamwork, so that's what I'm going to give him. Figure I might as well help you at the same time."

"I don't need help," I lied.

"You didn't look so hot the other night," he said. "And if I have to pass to someone, it might as well be you. How you handle the puck is up to you."

How could I refuse? We smacked gloves. Dillon had a dangerous side, but being his friend had its rewards. Besides, I needed to hang out with someone while I wasn't talking to Jason and Chen.

As we skated onto the ice, Ray Scott and the team trainer were setting up the nets. Skip was taking a few laps. His limp disappeared on the ice, and you could tell by the look in his eyes that hockey was in his blood.

"Hi, guys," he said, skating up to the group. "Nice to see all of you out tonight. During the first half of the session, I'm going to evaluate your skills and endurance. We're setting up an obstacle course. Good luck!"

Ray Scott, who insisted we call him "Scotty" gave us a quick rundown of the drill and then demonstrated by skating through the course.

At the sound of the whistle, I began doing crossovers around the face-off circle in my end. Next, I zig-zagged between orange cones making tight turns and controlling the puck. As I approached centre ice, I jumped over the red line, slid on my stomach, got up and recovered the puck. After that, I bolted to the far face-off circle to complete backward crossovers — my weakness. That's when Nitro flew past me and Marco approached, biting at my heels.

Coming out of the circle, I noticed the goalie was down, having just saved the previous player's shot. Skating in close, I flipped the puck over his shoulder and into the net. Raising my stick in the air, I cheered, making sure Skip had noticed. Dillon smacked my helmet. "Nice going."

The next drill was an endurance test. The coach instructed us to skate steady around the ends and sprint between the blue lines.

"A word of advice," Skip said. "Pace yourself. Otherwise you'll burn out."

At the whistle, I blasted off, ignoring his warning. This was my big chance, and I wasn't going to blow it. Coming up from the A/E team, I was an underdog. That meant I would have to push extra hard to impress the coaching staff.

With short, hard strides, I exploded ahead of the others. After five laps, the only skaters in front of me were Nitro, Marco and Dillon. I closed in on Marco, then powered my way past him. My thighs burned, but I kept pumping. My lungs burst for air, but I kept going. Then I got a stitch in my side. I tried to fight through it, but I felt my body slowing down.

Belch cruised by me. Then Marco skated alongside

me. He made a strange noise. Next thing I knew, he barfed on the ice — without breaking stride! Talk about tough. He must have wanted to make the team in a bad way.

The foul odor encouraged me to skate faster. Not fast enough though. Next thing I knew, Dillon came whistling up from behind. He was a *machine*, and he *lapped* me.

"Did you see that!" he exclaimed. "Marco tossed his cookies, and two guys skated through it."

"Looks like more than cookies," I said, gasping for air.

"You're falling behind," he warned. "I'll slow down and pace you."

"I can't go faster," I panted. "I've got a stitch."

"Push through the pain," he insisted. "It won't kill you."

Easy for a machine to say, I thought, grimacing.

As we approached the blue line, Dillon yelled, "Go! Go! Go!"

My legs wouldn't *go*. They wobbled under me like two deflated tires.

Dillon glanced behind. "Jason's gaining, and he looks good. You'd better watch out. You're competing for the same spot."

"Yeah," I puffed. "I know."

"Jason's coming up fast," Dillon observed. "And so is the blue line. Go! Go! Go!"

I dug my edges in, and pumped my legs hard. Even so, as I came out of the sprint, Jason glided past me.

"Hook him!" Dillon called. "Now!"

What can I say? I was desperate. And still angry. So it was easy. My stick came up and slipped around Jason's waist. One good yank threw him off balance. Down he tumbled like an uprooted tree. The coaches didn't even notice.

"Way to go!" Dillon congratulated me, as we skated past. "You didn't just slow him down, you took him out."

Jason deserved it. That's what I told myself. But I didn't dare look behind. Inside, I didn't feel good. I had crossed a line.

Fortunately, Scotty signaled the end of the drill a few minutes later. Any longer, and I would have collapsed. Everyone headed for the water bottles. Avoiding Jason, I sank down on the ice surface. My heart banged in my chest. I gasped for air. Guzzling some water, I began to recover.

Skip skated over to the group, looking concerned. "Are you okay, Marco?"

"Much better now," he replied, giving the coach the thumbs-up. "My grandmother made me eat a whole meatball sub before she drove me to the arena."

The poor guy next to me was frantically scrubbing his laces with wads of kleenex. I got off easy with a few splashes of tomato sauce up my socks. By the time the trainer cleaned up the remains of Marco's sub, we were set to scrimmage.

Dillon, Marco, Craig and I got handed white pinnies. Chen and Jason, Belch, and Nitro wore red. As in the previous tryout, we were going to play one-minute shifts, changing on the fly. It would be fast, intense action.

As I headed to the bench, Jason grabbed my arm, spinning me around. "Why'd you hook me?"

He caught me off guard. I didn't know what to say.

"You were right behind me," he said, his eyes raging. "It had to be you."

"Guess I wasn't watching my stick." A stupid answer and we both knew it.

"It felt like you knew what you were doing when you pulled me down."

"I was off balance."

The anger left his eyes. I think he believed me.

Before I could dig myself in deeper, Dillon called to me. "Let's go. We're on the first shift." As we skated into place, Dillon said, "Watch for my pass."

Nitro won the face-off. He slammed the puck to Jason who began stickhandling down the ice. Skating with the puck was Jason's weakness. He kept his head down as he struggled to stay in control, making himself an easy target. Sure enough, Dillon bulldozed him over at the blue line. Once Dillon got a hold of the puck, he started to skate, deking out Chen, and blasting right through the red squad's line of defence. He could have gone all the way, but instead he screeched to a stop, and passed the puck to me. On contact, I fired a snap shot at the net, sneaking the puck between the goalie's legs to score. Golden! The buzzer sounded. Dillon and I smacked gloves as we left the ice.

"Nice work," Skip said, as we filed past him.

Before long, he handed me another opportunity. Jason was skating along the boards with the puck. Dillon came angling in on him. Crunch! Leading with his shoulder, he smoked Jason into the boards. It was a hard but clean hit. Dillon fished the puck out from between Jason's skates and scrambled up the ice. He went the distance solo, hanging onto the puck until he saw me skating into the open. He delivered the puck straight to my tape. I curled behind the net, avoiding a check by Belch, and came out on the left side. As I attempted to tuck the puck into the corner of the net, the goalie's glove swept down and stopped it. The buzzer rang. I smiled to myself. No goal, but I had looked good.

Back on the bench, Skip walked over to Dillon. "That hit was almost boarding, son. The bodycheck is used to separate the opponent from the puck, not knock him out. Take it easy next time."

After the tryouts, the dressing room fell silent as we awaited the envelopes. Blood was seeping through

Dillon's bandage. He didn't complain, but I noticed he was limping.

Ever since I had hooked Jason, I had been feeling uneasy. I mean, Jason was a good friend, and I didn't want to screw that up. It had been one stupid moment.

Chen walked by me on his way to the showers. "How'd your new mouth guard work?" I asked, acting like my friendly old self.

"Get lost!" he replied, stone-faced.

What was his problem? All week he had been making a big deal about his dentist designing a new guard. And he didn't have to worry about making the team. He had played on the "A" team the previous season. Besides, coaches love Chen. He's a clean-hitting, hard working, high-scoring player.

Before I had a chance to talk to Jason, Skip entered the dressing room. He had traded his helmet for his ball cap. "Great job, everybody," he said. "You showed a lot of talent and determination. Those of you selected to continue trying out will compete in an exhibition game on Saturday afternoon against the Windsor Hawks. After that game, we'll make the final releases. Those of you not selected are invited to try-out for the A/E team, or you have the option of playing house league. Thank you, and have a good hockey season."

As we filed out the door, Skip handed out the

crisp, white envelopes. He instructed us not to open them until we were home. I made it to the car before I ripped mine open. Holding my breath, I read: *Congratulations! You are invited to the next tryout ...*

Yes! I had made the first cut.

9 Guilty as Charged

No one could catch me. I flew down the ice, faking out every player in my path. The opposition coach ordered a burly defenceman to take me out. The goon charged. A nanosecond before impact, I did a spin-a-rama around him. Dillon came pinching up on the offense. I slammed the puck to him, and he raced toward the net. Cutting into the open, I tapped my stick on the ice.

"Over here!" I shouted.

Dillon passed the puck.

"Matthew!" I heard Mom call.

Drawing back my stick, I prepared to onetime the puck into the net.

"Matthew, are you awake?"

I felt a hand on my shoulder, shaking me. "A boy is waiting for you at the front door," Mom said, snapping me into cold reality. "You're late for school."

"Why didn't you wake me?" I asked.

"I did," she replied. "You must have fallen back to sleep."

Rolling over in bed, I glanced at the clock: 8:40 a.m. Yikes! The school bell was set to ring in twenty minutes. Guess I forgot to set the alarm. Tryouts had wiped me out.

I searched the floor for some decent clothes, selecting a beige T-shirt with ancient pizza stains on one sleeve, and jeans with grass stains. Good enough, so long as Mom didn't get a close look. After a trip to the bathroom to slap down my bed-head, I grabbed my backpack and ran down the stairs.

There I found Dillon leaning against the screen door, chewing a wad of gum. He was wearing a black T-shirt with the word DESTRUCTION printed in bold letters across the front.

"What's with the *scare wear*?" I asked, as we walked down my driveway. "I can't believe your mom lets you wear shirts like that. Mine would toss it in the garbage."

He snapped his gum and laughed. "I bought it with my birthday money. Besides, my clothes are the least of her problems. Operation *Get Back To Toronto* is right on schedule. I should be home in time for Christmas."

"What have you been up to?" I inquired cautiously.

"Little things," he said, "like coming in past my curfew and using what Mom calls *foul* language. I keep telling her the kids from Lakeside are a bad influence on me. Soon, I'm going to step up the action. Think I'll start by getting suspended from school. That should rattle my parents' world. You know, I had the perfect chance that day — the fight. If only Kassy …"

I cut him off. "Hold on … I would have been suspended too."

"Lucky your girlfriend came to the rescue."

"She's not my girlfriend," I snapped back.

"If you say so …" He kept a straight face, but his eyes were dancing.

As we passed the mailbox, I realized Chen and Jason had left without me. My stomach tightened. "It's nothing," I told myself. Reaching deep into my back-pack, I pulled out a granola bar. We walked in silence while I ate. Finally, I blurted out what was on my mind. "I shouldn't have hooked Jason. That was low."

"Don't sweat it," Dillon said. "You'll never make a rep team if you play squeaky clean. Before each game, my old coach used to say, 'You're going into battle. Show no mercy. Remember, boys — no guts, no glory!'"

The man sounded like a military leader, not a hockey coach. Maybe he was the reason why Dillon thought it was okay to play rough.

"I told him it was an accident," I said.

"Don't worry," Dillon said, hitting my shoulder. "I won't say anything."

I studied his face for a moment and believed him.

A block from the school, the bell rang. We started to run. Dillon could hardly keep up. Although he didn't complain, his leg was obviously in bad shape.

At school, I fell into my desk, my legs burning from the sprint. Kassy poked me. When I turned, she batted her eyes at me and smiled. Her teeth were green.

"Whoa!" My head snapped back.

"Do you like my new braces?" she asked, drawing her lips back to give me a good view. "Green is my favourite — the colour of nature."

"They're very bright," I noted.

Actually, the green bands looked like bits of vegetables stuck between her teeth.

She tilted her head. "Will you sign my binder?"

"Uh, sure."

I grabbed a pen from my desk. "Don't sign it 'Goose,'" she instructed. "'Matthew' sounds more grown up."

Her binder was covered with poems and secret codes. Locating an empty space, I wrote "Matthew."

She wriggled her nose. "Is that all?"

What did she want from me? Feeling pressure, I added "ROCKS!" next to my name.

"Thanks!" She ran her fingers over my newly inked words. Then she leaned forward. "I've got an awesome idea. We could go to the movies. Just the two of us."

The movies … the two of us. It sounded like a–a … date!

"What about your parents?" I blurted. "They're Greek!"

"So what?"

"You told me Greek parents are strict. Your Dad won't let you date 'till you're sixteen. Huh? Remember?"

"Eighteen," she corrected me. "But it's different with you. My parents think you are responsible." She grinned. "Besides, they think we are just friends."

My stomach flipped. "But ... we are ... aren't we?"

"Of course," she said, her smile lingering.

Sitting there, stuck in my desk, with the teacher hovering close by, I felt trapped. Somehow I had to claw my way out.

"Uh ... I-I can't," I stammered. "I've got hockey."

She eyed me suspiciously. "The whole weekend?"

"Final cuts," I explained.

She touched my shoulder. "I understand. In soccer season, I'm busy every weekend. Don't worry, I'll think of something."

Yes! A clean escape.

After the morning announcements, Mrs. Carson instructed us to open our math textbooks. Geometry was a relief — much less complicated than my *friendship* with Kassy.

While the class was busy calculating angles, I tried to get Jason's attention. I needed to make sure we were still friends.

"Eyes on your work, Matthew," Mrs. Carson ordered, walking over me.

At recess I hurried to catch up with Chen and Jason as they headed down the hall.

"Wait up!"

The halls were a zoo. Chen and Jason couldn't hear me over the happy sounds of students who had just earned fifteen minutes of freedom. I caught up to my buds as they headed to the soccer field.

"Tryouts were brutal, eh?" I said, butting between them.

Jason stopped dead in his tracks. His eyes flashed. "You should know."

I took a step back. "Wh-what do you mean?"

Chen pointed an accusing finger at me. "I saw the whole thing. That was no accident."

"Why'd you do it?" Jason demanded.

"Uh, I-I don't know," I stammered. "It was crazy out there. I wasn't thinking …"

He cut me off. "Wrong! You were thinking — about making the team! I got cut last night. And it's *your* fault."

"No! You don't get it! I *want* to play together." A lump grew in my throat. "We'll go to the coach. I'll tell him what happened. I'll make it right."

Jason shook his head. "It's too late. I'm not crawling back to Skip."

"Okay, well, like, I'm sorry." My voice cracked. I

was almost bawling. "What are you going to do? Try out for the A/E team?"

He started to walk away "None of your business."

"Jerk!" Chen yelled, before running to catch up with Jason.

What had I done? Was making the team worth losing my friends? Walking off the field, I headed to the fence and slumped against the metal mesh. From there I watched the soccer game.

A chilling thought occurred to me — maybe, I didn't deserve a spot on the team.

10 The White Envelope

My sister, Julie, doesn't like cold arenas. She says they make her fingers go "dumb." And mittens interfere with the steady stream of finger foods Mom and Dad supply to keep her happy during a game. So, as usual, I found my family sitting in the bleachers beneath a glowing heater.

The exhibition game was about to begin. Twenty-two players had dressed to play. In one hour, seventeen would be left. Those players would make up the Lakeside Wave minor Pee Wee "A" team. The Windsor Hawks had traveled to Lakeside for the same reason: to see how their team responded in a game situation and to test what combination of players worked well together.

To my surprise, Skip put me on the starting lineup with Dillon. Guess he was impressed by our playmaking during the second tryout.

We took our positions on the ice. I tried to push Jason out of my mind, but it wasn't working. I couldn't help wondering which one of us would be here right now if I hadn't made him look bad during tryouts.

The two centres trained their eyes on the ref's hand. At the drop of the puck, Hawk's centre, number eight, drove it to his left winger. I charged after the winger, but before I could check him, he made a return pass to number eight. Dillon tried to poke-check it away, but number eight deked him out and skated down the wing. Suddenly, that wily centre was in position to take a shot on net. His stick went back. Wham! He hammered the puck toward the goal crease. Dillon dove to block the shot. In number eight, Dillon had finally met his match.

Skip made an adjustment to our line, putting Belch on defence with Dillon. Even with our strongest defensive line, most of the shift was played out in our end. Belch and Dillon worked hard clearing the puck and forcing number eight away from the net.

At the end of the shift, Skip patted our helmets. "Settle down, guys. Stick to the game plan."

I called down the bench to Dillon. "Who is that guy?"

"That guy is a girl. Chelsea Paterson. She played Triple A last year. We played against each other in a couple of tournaments."

I pounded my glove on the bench. "What's a girl doing out here?"

Dillon grinned. "She's making this game worth playing."

Chelsea Paterson dominated the first period. Dillon had his hands full playing defence. He didn't have time for any offensive playmaking. With fifteen seconds on the clock, Chelsea jumped in on a rebound, flipping the puck in the top corner of the net to score.

During the second period, Skip switched me to a different line. He brought Craig in to take my place. As I sat on the bench, my confidence sank.

The next time I got let out, Chen was carrying the puck down the neutral zone. A big Windsor player tried to knock him off the puck. Chen was thrown off balance, but somehow managed to hold on. Seeing an opening, he cut over along the boards. A Windsor defenceman angled in for the check, but at the last second, Chen spun around and passed the puck to Marco. Blam! Marco got bodychecked. On the way down, he took the other player with him.

"Loose puck!"

The race was on. Three of us closed in on the target. Someone's elbow spun me around. Another body collided into mine and we fell onto the puck. As I dug for the puck, some moron took his stick and slashed my calves. Clutching my legs, I rolled on the ice in agony. The whistle blew. The Windsor player received a two-minute penalty.

When the pain eased, I limped to the bench, glancing up at my family. Mom held her hand over her mouth. Dad was shaking his head. Julie was stuffing food in her mouth. Kassy was standing …

Kassy? Why was she at the game? Beside her sat Amy, looking bored. As I dragged myself to the bench, Kassy came running down the aisle. She stood behind me, calling over the glass, "Did he hurt you?"

A couple of the guys grinned at me.

This was not cool. If the team got this kind of ammunition, I'd be the butt of Craig's jokes. My hockey name would be Romeo.

I tried to ignore her, but she kept banging on the glass demanding, "Are you okay?"

Finally, I turned and gave a sharp, "No!"

"Good," she said, satisfied. "Meet me after the game. I need to talk to you."

The players grinned again. I dropped my head in my gloves, but then, I remembered the power play was about to begin. My mind shifted back to the game. Now that the Windsor Hawks were short-handed, maybe we could get some action around their net.

The Wave came on strong, with Kyle taking the puck across the blue line and shooting it ahead to Nitro. Craig tried to find an opening by the net, but the Hawk's had set up a tight box in front of their net. The puck went back and forth with no one shooting on net. Meanwhile, the penalty ticked down.

"Shoot! Shoot!" the crowd roared.

Suddenly, Chelsea intercepted the puck. She bolted out of their zone. A short-handed breakaway. No-o-o-o! I banged my stick on the boards. "Stop her!"

Dillon turned on the gas. As Chelsea closed in on our net, the goalie stood ready. She drew her stick back. Before she could follow through, Dillon reached out and hooked his blade around her waist, hauling her down on the ice. He prevented the goal. He also drew a penalty shot.

Both teams cleared the ice. Chelsea stood alone at centre ice, waiting to go one on one with our goalie. His name was Adam, and he had come up from house league. A house league goalie against a superstar! At least, it would be a quick slaughter.

Chelsea started up the ice, skating steady. Adam crouched low, waiting. She hesitated, then shot the puck. It went high and wide, hitting the glass. I couldn't believe my eyes.

"She panicked," Dillon explained. "It happens to the best."

In the final minutes of the period, both sides were playing short-handed due to penalties. We had the puck in their end and were passing back and forth when the Hawks' penalty ended. Marco didn't see the new skater until he came up from behind and poke-checked the puck into the open. A Windsor player carried the puck to the other end and scored, making it 2–0 for the Hawks.

Late in the third period, the score hadn't changed. Our team needed a couple of quick goals. Skip called a time out. "The game isn't over yet," he reminded us. "Time to talk strategy."

Armed with Skip's advice, the Wave pushed hard. I was skating with the puck, closing in on the Hawks' net. Seeing Chen in the open, I passed it to him. He looked like he was about to pass it, but instead he took a snap shot, catching the goalie by surprise. The puck slipped between his pads: five hole!

"Way to go!" I yelled.

A little over one minute showed on the clock. We could still tie. Skip assembled his best players on the ice. Nitro lost the face-off to Chelsea. She passed the puck to her teammate who skated into our zone. CR-U-NCH! Dillon took him out at the boards and stole the puck.

"Over here!" Nitro pounded his stick on the ice.

Dillon passed him the puck.

With forty seconds to go, Skip pulled our goalie, and sent Marco in. Nitro passed him the puck. Marco didn't see Chelsea coming at him until it was too late. Her solid bodycheck knocked him off his skates. As he fell, he took a wild shot. Unfortunately, a Hawk's defenceman picked up the puck. Chen raced in, pinning the guy against the boards. They fought for it, madly digging at the puck. I glanced up at the clock. Sixteen seconds. "C'mon, Chen!" I cried. "Knock it loose."

Chen managed to poke the puck out. Craig nabbed it, then wrapped around the net, leaning into a shot. Before he could tuck it in the net, the buzzer rang. The ref waved off the goal. Craig dropped to his knees in frustration. Final score 2–1 for the Hawks.

On our way to the dressing room, I met Kassy and Amy in the hallway. Belch greeted them with a burp.

"Gross!" Amy said, scrunching her nose.

"You're lucky all I brought up was air," Belch responded.

Kassy and Amy were not impressed. They glared at Belch. He didn't care.

Craig broke the icy tension with a joke. "What did the left skate say to the right?"

The girls shrugged.

"My, you're looking sharp tonight."

Amy volleyed a joke back at him.

Meanwhile, Kassy turned her attention to me. "Can you come for dinner tonight? My mom baked baklava … your favourite."

Baklava was the gooey Greek pastry made with honey and nuts. My mouth started to water. How could I say no? Still, if I said yes, what would that mean?

Fortunately, Dillon butted in. "Goose is going to the Junior B game with me tonight."

"Is that true?" she asked me, directly.

I gave an uneasy nod.

She sighed. "Some other time, I guess."

When Kassy left, I turned to Dillon. "Were you serious about the game?"

"Sure," he said. "My dad bought tickets. We were supposed to go together, but something came up at work. As usual, he can't make it."

I gave him a weak high-five. Normally, I'd be pumped to go to a Junior B game, but right then, something was weighing on my mind — my hockey future. There were four right wingers and the team needed three. What were my chances? Skip had pulled me off the line that faced Chelsea. He had seen me as a weak link. But I did get the assist on Chen's goal, and I didn't make any dumb mistakes.

I bent down on the bench to unlace my skates. That's when I noticed Dillon's leg. Fresh blood oozed through the bandage. "You should get that checked," I told him. "It's not healing."

"I'm fine," he said, grimacing. "Besides, what if the doctor says I can't play hockey?"

He had a point.

As we were getting changed, Skip came in and sat next to me, finishing up some paperwork. As he wrote, his ball cap bobbed under my eyes. Up close, I could make out some of the signatures: Bobby Hull; his son, Brett; Eddy Shack; Mats Sundin; Mario Lemieux;

Gordie Howe ... hockey legends — old and new.

"Nice hat!"

Skip smiled. "It inspires me on the bench."

The room grew quiet when Skip stood. "Such a pleasure working with you boys," he began. "I wish I could put each one of you on the team. All of you showed heart and determination ..."

My eyes concentrated on the envelopes in his hand.

When Skip finished his short speech, the players stood and received their envelopes as they filed out the door. My family was waiting down the hall. As I approached, Mom smiled and patted my back.

Dad used his words carefully. "Good work out there, son," he said, and nothing more. Even Julie knew enough not to speak. The moment had arrived ...

11 Flashback

The lights in the Shoreline Arena dimmed. The Junior B Wave's theme music began to play. It started as slow, rolling surf, steadily building into the thunderous roar of tidal waves. A burst of French horns from the loudspeakers sounded the arrival of the team. One after another, the players skated through a giant set of inflatable sturgeon jaws. The crowd cheered. I stood on my seat dancing. When Trent Sowinski skated out, I whistled and hooted.

"Get down, you geek!" Dillon barked.

My hands jabbed at the air. My body rocked. The people around me assumed I was an enthusiastic fan. Sure, Junior B hockey is cool, but it can't make me dance. The reason for my hyper feet — I had made the team!

The opposing team from Guelph skated onto the ice. The cheering subsided to a few polite claps.

"Sit down! You're blocking my view."

That voice — it sounded familiar. As I whirled around, a pair of glassy eyes met mine. Over two thousand people at the arena and Sophie Sterol *had* to sit behind me. My legs went limp.

"What are you doing here?" I demanded. "You don't even like hockey."

"Shows what you know," she said. "My dad and I have season's tickets."

Spike, the team's mascot came charging down our aisle, trying to excite the crowd.

"That's the fish from hockey camp!" Dillon exclaimed. "What's with a sturgeon for a mascot? Why not use something cool like a shark?"

"Excuse me," Sophie said, poking her head between us. "Sturgeons are over two hundred million years old. They were on earth before the dinosaurs."

"Maybe the sturgeon should be extinct, too," Dillon replied. "That is one ugly fish."

"You obviously don't know much about them," Sophie explained. "Sturgeons are the largest fish in the Great Lakes. Instead of scales, they have bony plates for protection."

Dillon twirled a finger in the air. "Who cares?"

"Our team doesn't need a man-eating fish to be cool," Sophie said, getting into a huff. "Besides, sharks are found in oceans. For your information, our team is the *Lakeside* Wave."

Dillon narrowed his eyes. "How do you know so much about the sturgeon?"

Before she could answer, I quipped, "Because they're related."

We turned back in our seats, cracking up. "Huh? What the —?" Cold liquid trickled down my forehead to my lips. I tasted Coke. Whipping around in my seat, I met Sophie's glare. She grasped the empty can in her hand.

"You asked for it!" I rose up in my seat, holding out my own drink, then reconsidered when I saw Mr. Sterol approaching with popcorn in his hands. Fuming, I sunk down in my seat.

After the national anthem, both teams took their positions at centre ice. I settled in to watch the game. It was fast playing and hard-hitting action. Those Junior B players were torpedoes on ice.

As the Coke dried on my face and neck, my skin became tight and sticky. My hair dried into hard clumps. Sophie had gone too far this time.

Near the end of a scoreless first period, Trent Sowinski intercepted a pass. Faking out the Guelph centre, he sped toward the boards. Their winger angled in on him. Trent accelerated, avoiding the check. Deep in the Guelph zone, a defenceman forced Trent away from the net. As Trent curled around the corner behind the goal, the defenceman stayed with him, poke-checking until the puck got jammed in one of

Trent's skates. He bent over to find it. At the same time, another Guelph player creamed him from behind. Trent flew headfirst into the glass, after which, he fell limp on the ice and lay motionless. The crowd gasped. An eerie silence followed.

The trainer sprang onto the ice. At once, he signaled to the team doctor. I kept my eyes trained on Trent, watching for a sign that he was all right. He didn't move.

"C'mon Trent," I murmured. "Get up!"

Nothing.

The doctor knelt down beside Trent, talking to him. No response. But wait — his right hand moved. He spoke. I started to breathe again.

A few minutes later, the large gate at the end of the arena opened. An ambulance backed up to the edge of the rink. Two paramedics carried a stretcher onto the ice. They fitted a neck brace on Trent, then carefully lifted him onto the stretcher. As he was carried to the waiting ambulance, the crowd stood and clapped to show their support.

"That sucks," Dillon said, "but it's part of the game."

I didn't comment. I was remembering hockey camp. The day I took the hit. The pain. The twinkling stars. I glanced back at Trent and grimaced. That could have been me.

The player who took out Trent was given a five-minute major and a game misconduct. The OHL would decide any further disciplinary action later. The Wave won 4–3. Considering what had happened to Trent, the win didn't seem all that important.

Sunday morning, I jumped on my bike and headed over to Dillon's to do math homework. Dillon was good at word problems. He showed me how to write each step of the problem down on paper. That way it's a lot easier to get the solution. Once we had finished our homework, we shot baskets on his driveway. Dillon could be a nice guy when he wasn't working at being bad.

That evening, the radio replayed highlights of the Junior B game while I snacked on leftover pizza. The announcer gave an update on Trent's condition. He had been unconscious for two minutes — it had seemed more like five. He would be out for an undetermined amount of time. That could mean weeks or months. The announcer went on to discuss concussions in hockey and how the problem is increasing even though players wear better protective equipment. Brain injury has ended brilliant NHL hockey careers. The announcer invited the listeners to call in and give their opinions as to why this is happening. But I didn't stick around to hear because I had finished the pizza.

12 Second Chances

Monday morning, Mrs. Carson sent the class to the library to research Canada's aboriginal people. Selecting an encyclopedia, I settled into a chair to read about the Iroquois tribes.

Miss Bates, the librarian, stood behind me, her vanilla perfume wafting through my nostrils, making me crave cookies.

"Better get something down on paper," she instructed, over my shoulder. "You have forty minutes in which to complete your research."

I began to write notes on the Iroquoian long-houses. Satisfied, Miss Bates returned to her computer and disappeared behind the screen. Dillon came along and sat next to me. "Payback time," he whispered.

"Huh? I don't owe you."

"Sophie," he explained. "You're not going to let her get away with dumping a Coke on you … are you?"

An uneasy feeling gripped me. "What are you thinking?"

Smirking, he wadded up a piece of paper and popped it in his mouth.

"Spitballs!" I said, catching on. "Good and germy. Sophie will freak."

"Watch this!" he said, loading an empty pen cartridge, then firing. Bull's-eye! Sophie swatted her neck. "Something bit me!"

Miss Bates walked over to her. "Let me have a look," she said, putting on her glasses.

Sophie craned her neck to one side. "Is it bleeding?"

Miss Bates took a close look. "You are fine, Sophie. I don't see a mark."

"I'm not making it up!" Sophie insisted, her voice cracking.

"Calm down," Miss Bates said, firmly.

Dillon and I nearly split our guts laughing. Only Sophie would freak out over a little spitball.

Miss Bates got the class's attention. "I'll be gone for a few minutes. I need some printer paper from the supply room."

With Miss Bates out of the way, we took turns firing spitballs at Sophie's hair. She didn't notice — until Amy clued her in.

"Hold still," Amy said, "I'll get rid of them."

Sophie grabbed Amy's arm. "Don't touch them with your bare hands! Do you have any idea how many germs are in human saliva? Dogs have cleaner mouths."

Kassy laughed. "You wouldn't say that if you saw what my dog ate at the schoolyard the other day."

Sophie's clapped her hand over her mouth. "What did Chico eat?"

"Someone dumped the garbage can by the swings," Kassy said. "It was filled with old school lunches. Fuzzy bread, green meat, sour chunks of milk — all covered in maggots. But even rotting food smells good to a dog. To Chico's nose, it smells like a gourmet feast."

Sophie turned sickly white. "Stop! I can't listen. Chico is such a smart poodle. Why would she ..."

Miss Bates returned with a stack of paper. Sophie didn't waste any time. "I was attacked with spitballs," she blabbed, pointing directly at us. "They did it!"

Miss Bates glared. "I'll deal with the two of you once I put the paper away."

Dillon shoved an elbow in my ribs. "Quick! Eat the evidence."

"But ...what if I choke?"

"Chew!" Dillon ordered.

Since I didn't have a better idea, I shoveled nine spit-balls in my mouth, carefully tucking them in my cheeks.

Once Miss Bates had calmed Sophie, she marched over to us. "Well, boys, do you have anything to say in your defence?"

Dillon pasted on an angelic smile. "We were doing our work." He held up his research paper. He had written two sentences. Mutely, I held up my six lines of work. I didn't speak for fear I would spill the balls.

A vein bulged in Miss Bates' forehead. "I don't have time to play detective. You two may discuss this with the principal. I will inform Mr. LaFond that you are on your way."

Miss Bates returned to her desk and picked up the phone. Sophie excused herself to the washroom. As Dillon and I headed out the door, he lifted Sophie's research papers from the table.

"What a laugh!" Dillon said, on our way to the office.

Getting sent to the principal didn't seem funny to me. I walked silently beside him. As we approached the boys' washroom, he pulled me in. I stared in disbelief as he tossed Sophie's research papers into a toilet and flushed. "Bye, bye!" he called to the swirling notes.

Seconds later, the toilet choked on the papers. Water gushed, higher and higher, until it reached the lip, and came raining down on my running shoes. We high-tailed it out of there. Dillon laughed like crazy. But I knew we were in big trouble.

★ ★ ★

Mrs. Milson, the school secretary, was sitting at her desk in the outer office when we arrived. "Good morning, Dillon," she said, with a knowing look. "Are you here to see Mr. LaFond?"

He shook his head. "I didn't do nothin'."

"You mean I didn't do *anything*." She pointed to principal's door. "You may enter."

Mrs. Milson smiled at me. "How may I help you, Matthew?"

"Uh … I'm with him."

"Fine. In you go." Her smile shrunk a size.

Taking a deep breath, I followed Dillon into the office. Mr. LaFond looked up from his desk. "Hi, boys," he said, observing us through his thick glasses. "Please, sit down." He motioned to the straight-back chairs opposite his desk.

I sat down, gripping the sides of my chair.

Our school records lay on his desk. While he read through them, I discovered a ragged fingernail to gnaw on. When he finished, he fixed his eyes upon me. "Matthew, this sort of behavior seems unusual for you. Your records do not indicate any previous trouble." His microscope-like lenses bore down on me, causing me to shrink. "Let's talk about what happened in the library."

Talk was dangerous. I didn't want to lie. But if I told the truth, I would implicate Dillon. And that was not safe.

When I didn't say anything, the principal leaned forward in his chair, closing the gap between us. "Well…?"

"Sophie's the one with the problem," Dillon piped up. "She dumped a Coke on Matt."

Mr. LaFond didn't seem interested in following up with Dillon. He kept his focus on me. My eye twitched. The pressure was getting to me. I was about to break. "It was …" Dillon grabbed my arm and squeezed.

"Yes," Mr. LaFond said, observing Dillon's grip on me. "Go on."

"I fired the spitballs at Sophie," I confessed.

"Very well." He appeared satisfied. "Dillon, you may return to the library."

"But —" he started to protest.

"That is all," Mr. LaFond said, ushering him out.

I sat alone, awaiting my fate.

Mr. LaFond returned to his desk. "Now that we are alone, is there anything you wish to tell me in confidence?"

I shifted uncomfortably. "Ummm … no."

"Protecting Dillon will not help him."

A long silence followed. He studied my face carefully. Then, to my surprise, he stood and shook my hand. "Doing the right thing takes courage," he said. "If you ever want to talk — about anything — come and see me."

I couldn't believe the principal was setting me free. At the very least, I expected serious detention time. As he ushered me out, he said, "I allow each student one free pass. Do you understand?"

I nodded. Mr. LaFond was giving me another chance. One thing for sure — I didn't want to end up in the office again. Suddenly, I got a sick feeling. What if Mr. LaFond found out about the incident in the boys' washroom? What would I do then? How far would I go to protect Dillon?

13 Playing with the Lions

On Saturday afternoon the newly formed team arrived at the Shoreline Arena. During the mid-week practices, Skip had worked us hard in preparation for the first regular season game. We had chosen our captain, Nitro; and the two assistant captains, Chen and Belch. The Lakeside Wave was ready to play the London Lions.

In the dressing room, Dillon sat next to me, inspecting a skate blade. Lately, things had changed between us. We had been getting along more like real friends. He had even dropped the tough-guy attitude around me. Somehow, I think Dillon knew that he had gone too far at school, and was lucky I was still his friend. All along, something had been bothering me, but I hadn't said a word. I had let it smolder. Not any longer. Like I said, things had changed between us. I was ready to stand up to him.

"I don't get it," I said, adjusting an elbow pad. "You

wanted to get suspended, and you had the perfect opportunity. So, why'd you let me take the fall?"

He put his skate down. "Oh, come on! You're not supposed to confess. That's not how the game works."

Game? Was lying to the principal his idea of fun?

I said, "My parents would freak if I got suspended. They might even pull me off the team. So next time, leave me out."

He snapped his towel at my face. "Get real! You wanted to get back at Sophie. Don't deny it."

He had a point. Firing spitballs at Sophie had been the highlight of my week. Still …

Craig broke the tension with a fresh joke. "Why do the London Lions wear long underwear?"

Dillon and I shrugged.

"Because they freeze when they hit the ice."

My new Wave jersey was aqua with a white tidal wave on the front and the number sixteen. As I wrestled it over my shoulder pads, a fresh scent filled my nose. A little game sweat would take care of that. Just then, Adam walked in. The rookie goalie had made the team.

Skip stopped by and announced last minute adjustments to the lineup. "I want you to remember three things," he said. "Play as a team, avoid unnecessary penalties and respect the other players. Play clean."

Scotty poked his head in the door. "Game time."

As we headed out of the dressing room, Chen pushed passed me. Dillon stopped by the door and grabbed a stick — a brand new, one-piece composite stick — every hockey player's dream. "Wicked!" I exclaimed. "Where did you get that?"

He held it protectively. "My dad got it in Toronto. I can't wait to test this baby."

Two minutes into the game Dillon got his chance. Controlling the puck, he skated behind our net, then up along the boards to the blue line. When he saw a Lion closing in, he pushed the puck ahead, spun around the confused player, and picked it up on the other side. Increasing his speed, he flew across the neutral zone to the Lion's blue line where he came to a screeching halt. From the point, he slammed a wicked slapshot. It sizzled toward the top right corner of the net. The goalie couldn't react fast enough. Dillon scored!

At the line change, I skated to the face-off circle with Nitro and Chen. Something made me look up. I thought I saw Jason walk into the arena. On second thought, it was someone with the same coat.

Forget him, I told myself. Concentrate on the game.

I shifted my eyes back to the puck.

Nitro was explosive in the face-off. He slammed the puck out of the circle to Chen. Two Lions closed in on Chen. In response, he fired the puck to me. I picked it up and began stickhandling up the boards. I heard the crowd cheering me on … or wait — it was the coach shouting at me. "Heads up!"

Too late. Wham! I got slammed into the boards. The puck disappeared. The Lion winger who had hammered me rushed with the puck into our end. As he closed in on the net, Adam crouched down low. Two Lions roamed in front of the crease, screening our goalie. The winger let go a hard wrist shot. Adam fell to his knees and blocked the shot. A close call.

As I left the ice, Skip, patted my helmet, "Good work, son. Remember to keep your head up."

Good work! I nearly handed the other team a goal.

Part way into my next shift, Dillon came in on the fly. My confidence returned. Dillon got hold of the puck and rushed across centre ice, deking out every Lion in his path. He roared across the blue line, then swept the puck up the ice to me. I snapped my bottom wrist, letting go a hard shot. I drove it straight between the goalie's legs to score. The crowd cheered. I could hear my dad's shrill whistle above the clapping. My teammates skated over, slapping my helmet.

Back on the bench, I aimed the water bottle down my throat. The goal was just what I needed. I was back in the game.

Early in the second period, the Lions pounced, scoring with a sneaky wraparound goal. Shortly after that, Dillon got called for slashing and spent two minutes in the box. The Lions scored on the power play, and suddenly the game was tied 2–2.

The Lions kept advancing. Our defence worked

hard clearing the puck. Before long, Belch grew dead tired defending our end. Skip called him off and sent in Dillon.

As the Lion centre sped toward our net, Dillon cut in front of him. Crouching low, he delivered a solid hipcheck. The surprised Lion somersaulted over Dillon's back and crashed onto the ice, loosing his stick. Meanwhile, a Lion winger nabbed the puck and skated behind the net. Dillon got up and charged, crushing the Lion into the end boards. The dazed player dropped to the ice. The whistle blew. The ref signaled "boarding."

Staggering to his feet, the London player skated slowly to the bench. The poor guy — getting crunched by the machine.

The ref handed Dillon a two-minute penalty. After serving his time in the box, Skip benched him for another five minutes. I don't know who was angrier — Skip or Dillon.

In the third period, the action went back and forth between ends. Neither team could gain the advantage. That changed during the last two minutes of the game when a Lion player got called for tripping. Craig scored with a backhand on the power play. With forty-five seconds left, the Lions pulled their goalie. They came on strong, taking five quick shots on net. At the same time, we fell apart, panicking, and forgetting to play our positions. In the end, we got lucky.

The buzzer came to our rescue. Final score: 3–2: Wave.

Back in the dressing room, Skip handed out the fall schedule. My eyes widened when I noticed an early season tournament in Waterloo, Ontario. That meant two nights in a hotel — hopefully one with a swimming pool — and eating fast food … I could hardly wait!

14 Bent out of Shape

On Monday morning, Sophie got called down to the office. She returned a few minutes later with a smug grin. I shifted uneasily in my desk.

Mrs. Milson's voice came ringing through the P.A. system: "Kassy Laskaris, please report to the office."

Ten more students got summoned. What was going on? I didn't have to wonder for long. When Kassy returned, she pointed an accusing finger at me. "Was it you?"

"Huh?" My stomach flipped.

"Did you flush Sophie's research down the toilet?"

"No, it wasn't me!"

"Okay," she said, watching me carefully. "I believe you."

Mrs. Milson's voice came over the P.A. system. "Matthew Gander, please report to the office."

My heart started to pound as I began the terrible

trek to the office. What would I say? How much did the principal know?

I found Mr. LaFond sitting at his desk. He regarded me grimly. "I was hoping we wouldn't meet like this so soon."

I sat down, rocking nervously in the chair.

Mr. LaFond drew his dark brows together. Behind his thick glasses, his eyes pinned me. I looked down at his desk, unable to hold his glare.

"Someone flooded the boys' washroom last Wednesday — about the time you and Dillon were on your way to the office. After the janitor fixed the toilet, he brought me a convincing bit of evidence — wet papers upon which Sophie Sterol's name appeared in ink. I had to attend a conference on Thursday and Friday, which gave me time to think." He paused.

My cheeks burned.

Then he asked the dreaded question. "Were you involved?"

My mouth went dry.

"Matthew," he said, finally, "Shall I interpret your silence as an admission of guilt? I hope you understand the gravity of this offence. You could be facing a suspension."

Suspension? What would my parents say? No! I wouldn't go down like this!

"I-I didn't do it," I choked out. "It wasn't me. Honest, Mr. LaFond!"

I expected him to pressure me — force me to rat out Dillon. Instead, he stood and shook my hand. "Thank you," he said. "You may return to your classroom."

Back in class, I couldn't concentrate. Dillon hadn't been called to the office yet. What would he say? Would he implicate me?

I hammered on his back. "The principal's going to question you about the flooded toilet. He's got evidence — Sophie wrote her name on the papers."

Dillon whirled around in his desk. "What did you tell him?"

"Nothin'… except that I didn't do it."

He knocked himself in the head. "How could I have been so stupid?"

"I'm not taking the fall," I warned him. "Not this time."

Was it my imagination, or did I see fear in his eyes?

Just then, Dillon got called to the office. I waited in a sweat. Minutes passed, then hours. By lunch recess, rumor spread that he had been suspended.

I felt lousy for the rest of the day — tired, achy, miserable. After school, I high-tailed it over to his house. No one answered. I noticed the door was slightly ajar, so I poked my head in, and called, "Hey, Dillon, are you home?"

"Up here," he answered.

I found him lying on his bed, sketching a picture of a two-headed monster.

"Self portrait?" I joked.

He didn't laugh.

I stood rigid against the door. "Is it true? Did you get suspended?"

"For two days," he said, keeping his eyes trained on the monster.

"What happened?"

"Mr. LaFond isn't stupid," he said. "One piece of the puzzle was missing. He wasn't sure if I acted alone. I told him the truth — you had nothing to do with it."

"That's great!" I exclaimed, punching the air. "You wanted a suspension."

He dropped his sketchpad and rolled over, burying his head in his pillow. "My mom's making me see a counsellor. She's searching for one right now."

"Oh," I said, sensing the subject was off bounds. "Well, what about Toronto?"

"Nothing is turning out the way I expected," he muttered into the pillow.

Obviously Dillon wanted to be alone, so I left him with his monster.

When I got home, the phone was ringing.

"Hello," I answered.

"You were mean to Sophie!" an angry voice shouted in my ear. "Spitballs! Why did you do it?"

"She deserved it!" I shot back. "She dumped a Coke on my head."

Kassy let out a loud huff. "Because you said she was related to a fish. You should apologize."

"No way," I said, accidentally snorting into the receiver.

"Then you're a jerk." And before I could reply, she hung up.

A few minutes later, Mom appeared at my bedroom door with Julie in tow. "Matt, would you please entertain your sister while Dad and I make supper?"

"Not now!" I was already in a lousy mood. Besides, I had a headache and my throat felt weird.

"We'll play ponies," Julie suggested eagerly.

"No!" I protested. "Not ponies! Anything but ponies."

★ ★ ★

Julie grabbed the white pony. "I get to be Samantha, the Rainbow Wonder." She dropped the chestnut-coloured stallion on the carpet in front of me. "You be Cory. He's the farm horse."

"Sure, sure … whatever," I said, bored out of my skull.

"Help! Help!" Samantha whinnied from the edge of the sofa. "I'm falling off the cliff. Hurry, Cory!"

I let out a sickly, "Neigh! Neigh! Here comes Cory to the rescue."

Cory hobbled up the sofa. When he reached the top, he went through an amazing transformation. The fat farm horse turned into Thug, the Thunder Stallion. Wham! With a cruel thrust, he pushed Samantha off the cliff to the raging river below.

Julie's face fell. "Matt!" she said, "You're the meanest brother in the whole world! You hurt Samantha — on purpose!"

"I was just trying to make the game more interesting."

"Daddy!" Julie called. "Matt's …"

I pulled her down wearily. "Fine, we'll play your way."

"Goody," she said smugly. "This time Cory falls off the cliff, and Samantha comes to the rescue."

"Whatever." I knew dinner would be ready soon, and later, I could escape to the arena.

As it turned out, practice was a bust. I could hardly keep up with the team. That night, I developed a fever, and lay freezing under a pile of blankets. It hurt to swallow, and my head pounded. The next day I stayed home sick. Mom gave me regular doses of Tylenol and ginger ale. Then, she booked a doctor's appointment for the next day.

"Open wide," Dr. Wilson said, as I gagged on the long cotton throat swab. "Might be a strep infection," he concluded, "but I want to be certain before I prescribe an antibiotic."

"What's the fastest cure?" I asked. "I've got a hockey tournament in two days."

"The results should be in on Friday," he said. "If it's a virus, you will probably feel better on your own by then. However, if the infection is bacterial, the results of the swab will let me know which drug to prescribe."

"I can't be sick!" I insisted. "I gotta play."

Dr. Wilson smiled sympathetically, but couldn't cure me.

On Friday morning, Dr. Wilson's office called. The results had come back positive for strep A. That meant I needed a prescription.

"I can still make the tournament," I tried to convince Mom. "A few doses, and I'll feel fine."

Mom put a hand on my shoulder. "I've already phoned your coach and explained that you are sick. Even if you start to feel better by tomorrow, you will be too weak to play hockey. Besides, strep throat is contagious. It wouldn't be fair to expose the rest of the team."

"Fair!" I roared. "*This* is no fair!"

Stomping upstairs, I slammed my bedroom door behind me and stayed there until I got hungry.

On Sunday night, Dillon phoned with a rundown of the tournament. "It was awesome! We played four games and ended up tied for second. Each player received a medal."

"Great," I said. But inside, I was growing sour.

"The hotel had a pool and a hot tub," he went on. "The coaches arranged a pizza party on Saturday night."

I was about to explode, when Dillon's tone suddenly changed. "There's something else. Skip called my parents and me to his hotel room. He was upset over a few penalties."

I gripped the phone tightly. "What kind?"

"I don't get the coach," he said. "I worked hard."

"So what happened?" I asked.

"Okay," he said. "In the first game, I gave some guy a clean check. It wasn't my fault the guy didn't know how to take a hit. Anyway, he separated his shoulder, and I got called for boarding. I felt bad — seriously. I didn't mean to hurt him. Anyway, Skip was ticked, so I slowed down in game two. But, by game three, the competition was tough, and I wasn't the only one throwing my weight around." He hesitated.

"Yeah," I said impatiently, "go on."

"I ended up in the box for roughing and slashing."

"Skip must have been on the warpath," I commented.

"They were tough games," Dillon snapped. "What was I supposed to do — sit back and watch them win?"

"Wish I was there," I said, trying to imagine it.

"So," he went on, "in the fourth game, we were tied. The championship was on the line. With six minutes left, a guy from the other team tripped me. The whistle blew, and the ref gave *me* the penalty. I admit I got carried away, busting my chops at him. Next thing I know, he handed me a misconduct."

"Whoa!"

"The thing is, if I had been in the game for the last couple of minutes, we would have won. Not that Skip cared. He threatened to release me if I don't play by his rules." Dillon gave an uneasy laugh. "But I'm not worried — I got four goals and seven assists. Skip can't get rid of me. I'm too good."

15 Pass the Ketchup

"Liar!"

I turned to face my accuser.

"You swore you didn't flush Sophie's papers! So why'd you get suspended? Eh? Eh? Eh?" Kassy repeated, jabbing a finger in my face.

"I was at home sick," I replied.

"And I should believe you because —?"

"Because it's true!" I fired back. Just then, I glanced down at her binder. My name had been blotted out with a blue marker. The name "Jimmy" had been freshly enclosed in a pink heart.

"Who's 'Jimmy'?" I asked.

"None of your business," she said. A smile creased her face. "Why? Are you jealous?"

"No," I replied quickly. "Just wondering."

"All right, so you didn't get suspended," she said. "Why haven't you apologized to Sophie yet?"

Ignoring her, I turned to face the front.

Kassy hammered on my back. "Just because you don't like Sophie, doesn't give you the right to pick on her."

"Why do you care?" I asked, getting annoyed. "It's not like you two are best friends."

"When did you become so *mean*?" she said, shaking her head.

"Okay," I said, taking a deep breath. "If it makes you happy, I'll apologize."

At recess I found Sophie playing foursquare on the tarmac with a group of girls. When she got "out," I walked up to her.

"Sorry," I said. "About everything." As I spoke the words, I realized I meant them. I was sick of our war.

She tugged on her ear. "I haven't exactly been nice to you, either," she admitted.

"Dumping that Coke on my head was pretty low," I pointed out.

She laughed. "It made nasty looking hair gel."

I hesitated, then said, "Truce?"

"Truce." Sophie reached out and shook my hand, missing my wart by a centimeter. She didn't flinch. She smiled at me. For the first time, I noticed her eyes were sea blue. My face burned. I ran to the soccer field.

Back in the classroom, Kassy pounded on my back. "That must have been a good apology," she said. "Not only does Sophie forgive you, but, well, there's more." Grabbing my binder, she wrote:

Sound the trumpet,

Sound the flute,

Sophie Sterol,

Thinks you're cute.

My head dropped. "You're kidding, right?"

"Seriously," Kassy said, "Sophie thinks you've changed, for the better. If you got that wart removed, she might … well, you know … like you." She studied my face. "Would you like her back?"

"What? No!"

I glanced over at Sophie. She smiled at me.

This called for drastic measures. Putting my finger to my lips, I planted a long, lingering wet one on my wart. "Buddy, old pal," I murmured, lovingly, "we're together forever."

From across the room, I saw Sophie's face scrunch up, and heard her go "Eww … disgusting."

Mission accomplished.

"Matt … M-a-a-tt! You aren't listening. I'm trying to tell you something important."

I gave Kassy my full attention.

"I think we should be just friends," she said. "I'm not ready for a boyfriend."

My insides leaped for joy. Then I remembered the other guy. "What about Jimmy?" I pointed to her binder.

"Oh, him." She blushed. "He's the star of *Zoo Crew*, that new show on TV, you know, where the kids act like animals to win prizes."

Girls? They were a mystery. Hockey was all I needed. At least there were rules.

★ ★ ★

Thursday night we faced off against the Leamington Reds. Before the game, Dillon pulled back his bandage to show me the wound. It was milky white with an angry red border. A few of the metal stitches had popped.

Staring down, I thought I was going to barf. "Shouldn't the staples be out by now?" I asked.

"Yeah, but look, it's not healing."

"Isn't your mom worried?"

"Not really. I keep it covered and I tell her that it's fine. I also told her the staples come out in four weeks, not two, like the doctor said. It doesn't hurt … much."

"Maybe not," I said, "but you shouldn't mess around with that. I heard about this guy who got a bug bite that got infected. He let the infection grow until his leg blew up like a balloon." Slicing my hand through the air, I delivered the grim news: "The doctor had to amputate."

"Really?" he said, his eyes bulging.

"Honest. I saw it on TV."

The colour drained from his face. Maybe I finally got to him.

Kyle called from across the room. "Does anyone

know why the Leamington team is called the Reds?"

"That'll be the colour of their faces when we whomp 'em," Craig quipped.

"My family visited Leamington last year," Marco said, while he taped his socks. "It's the tomato capital of Canada. In the fall, trucks carry tons of tomatoes to the Heinz factory. The town even has a tomato stomping contest!"

"Hope those tomatoes don't end up as ketchup," Kyle said, sticking out a dirty foot.

"Mmmm …" Craig said. "Toe jam ketchup."

During the pre-game warm-up, I spotted my family in the bleachers. Mom and Dad were talking to Mrs. McPhail. Julie was running up and down the stairs playing tag with another little kid.

The Leamington team wore white jerseys with a big red tomato on the front. Craig came up with some funny lines about "squashing the tomatoes" and "making sauce out of the Reds." Deep down though, I like tomatoes. I mean, what would fries and burgers be without ketchup?

After the pre-game handshake, I skated to the bench. Nitro lost the face-off. Determined to recover the puck, our captain shot off like a cannon after a Reds' winger and poke-checked him. The puck dribbled into the open. Craig scooped it up, but with two Reds covering him, he slipped the puck to Chen. Closing in on the net, Chen took a shot. It hit the goalie's shoulder and bounced outside the goal crease. Nitro dove for the rebound, sliding across the ice. Reaching out with his stick, he jabbed the puck toward the net. The Leamington goalie slid down, trapping the puck under his pads.

The Wave fired shot after shot on the Reds' net. Their goalie flopped all over the ice like a fish. Although he didn't look graceful, he did manage to save every shot.

During the line change, Craig slapped my helmet. "Go get 'em."

Marco passed to me. The puck glanced off the end of my blade and slid directly to a Reds' player. The guy dropped the puck off to his teammate who slipped in front of our net and scored. Dropping my head in disgrace, I skated off the ice.

The teams were evenly matched. The action shifted back and forth from end to end with both sides keeping up the pressure. Then two players got tied up at the boards. Dillon came up from behind and jabbed the puck out from under them. Seeing an opening, he skated up the middle, then veered to the right. At the point, he drew his composite stick high over his head and blasted a slapshot. The Reds' goalie reached out and caught the puck in his glove. Even Dillon's speeding rocket couldn't get past him. We were beginning to fear the Leamington goalie was unbeatable, when Kyle wrapped around the net and slipped the puck into the corner. At the end of the first period the game was tied 1–1.

During the second period, we got some bad breaks. The puck hit the goalpost on one scoring attempt and the crossbar on the next. Chen got slashed in a pileup in front of the net, but didn't draw a penalty, as the ref hadn't seen the offence. The ref did manage to catch all of our infractions. Dillon got called for roughing when he hauled some guy down on the ice. Marco got a penalty for hooking. Belch got one for holding. As for me: I deserved the Dumb Penalty award. I was skating fast after a Leamington winger, swinging my stick from side to side instead of keeping it down in front of me. I tripped the guy and got a two-minute penalty. Skip was not impressed, especially when the Reds scored on the power play. I had messed up twice, handing the opposition scoring opportunities.

"Don't worry about it," Skip told the team. "We've got the third period to make a comeback. Stay calm and play your positions."

The home crowd cheered, "Go, Wave, Go!" Our fans wanted a goal. Chen pinned a Reds' winger to the boards in our end. Both players dug wildly for the puck. Finally the winger knocked it out with his foot, handing it straight to Belch. Racing behind our net, Belch swept the puck out to Craig. Heavily guarded, Craig dumped the puck to Nitro who blasted off down the ice. A stocky defencemen cut in to take out

Nitro, but before he could, Nitro slammed a shot. He scored!

Four minutes on the clock. The game was tied 2–2. We needed a goal. And I needed to prove to Skip — and myself — that I could play hockey. The thing is, I couldn't shake off the guilt over what I did to Jason. It was crippling my game. If it weren't for Dillon setting me up, and making me look half-decent, Skip would have benched me long ago.

My eyes locked on the Reds' left winger as he stickhandled along the boards. I angled in, going for the check, knees bent, head up — perfect technique. But wait! At the last second, he accelerated, and I went slamming into the boards. Ugghh! That hurt! Meanwhile, he skated off toward our net.

Skip substituted Dillon on the fly. He charged, aiming to plow down the left winger. At the same time, the Leamington centre headed for Dillon. The three collided, full force. The winger slid across the ice, Dillon fell forward, and the centre landed on top of him. Shoving the player off, Dillon scrambled to his feet. There, on the ice, lay his stick in two pieces. Dillon kicked the ice. He yelled something, then dropped his gloves and took a swing at the stunned centre. The player refused to fight back. Dillon took another swing and yelled something at the ref.

"You're outta here!" the ref called. "A five-minute major for roughing and a game misconduct."

Dillon stormed to the dressing room, banging and crashing all the way.

Skip dropped his head for a moment. Then he tipped back his ball cap and called a time out. "Two minutes are left in the game and we're short-handed," he told the team. "Let's hold onto the tie. Keep in a tight box formation, forcing the opposition away from the net. I want to see strong, defensive hockey."

Skip sent his best players to the ice. I watched from the bench as the Reds came at us full force. With less than a minute to go, our defensive box fell apart. The Wave scrambled, trying to block the Reds' passes. It looked more like a game of monkey-in-the-middle than hockey. The Reds fired on our goalie from the point; they zinged shots in from the sides.

With ten seconds left in the game, their centre closed in on our net. He shot wide. Their winger picked up the puck, wrapped around our net, and tried to sneak it into the corner. Adam fell on his back, miraculously deflecting the shot, but putting himself out of position. A Reds' winger picked up the rebound. He took a shot, aiming it at the left corner of the net. There was no way Adam could stop the goal. Belch dove. The puck glanced off his ankle. He rolled on the ice in pain, no doubt his ankle swelling in shades of red and blue. A bruise was a small sacrifice. Belch was a hero. We held onto the tie.

16 Skip's Office

"My stick! He broke my new one-piece." Dillon sat slumped over on the bench in the dressing room.

"Good work out there," Skip told the team. Usually, Skip had more to say, but this time, he simply walked over to Dillon and said, "Come with me." On the way out of the dressing room, Skip tapped me on the shoulder. "Matt, come to the coaches' room once you get undressed."

Craig walked up to me with a stupid grin on his face. "What did the player say when the ref called 'icing'?"

I ignored him.

"Where's the cake?" He slapped my back. "Get it?"

"It's not funny!" I snapped back.

Craig shot me a look, then walked to the opposite bench.

"What's with you?" Nitro said. "He was just having fun."

I dropped my head. "Skip wants to see me."

"Oh." Nitro put a hand on my shoulder. "It's not what you think."

I finished getting changed, then gathered my equipment and headed down the hall. As I approached the coaches' room, the door flew open. Dillon charged out, knocking me aside. Mrs. McPhail followed, wiping her eyes. Skip stood in the doorway, stone-faced.

"Come in, Matthew," he said, quietly.

Skip sat down. He removed his ball cap and placed it on the desk.

"You wanted to see me?" I asked, limply.

"Sit down," he said, motioning to a chair. Some of my teammates entered the hallway, laughing and carrying on. "Perhaps you could close the door first."

I did as he said, then sat. That's when I noticed Scotty sitting at a table across the room, doing some paperwork. He looked up and gave me an awkward smile.

Just get it over with, I thought.

"During tryouts you seemed full of drive and determination," Skip began. "Lately, I sense a change. Are you still rundown from the strep throat?"

"No, I'm okay."

He leaned forward. "Is something bothering you?"

The office — the talk. This felt familiar. My mind flashed back to the principal's office. I remembered

Mr. LaFond saying, "It takes courage to do the right thing."

That time, I got a second chance.

"I did something —" I began, then stopped. Maybe full confession wasn't such a bright idea. After all, why should I hand Skip one more reason to get rid of me?

"Go on," Skip urged.

"It's nothing." Not daring to meet his eyes, I focused on his ball cap instead, studying the signatures.

"Even the hockey 'greats' make their share of mistakes," Skip said. "But they don't let anything stop them from achieving their goals."

What would they do? I asked myself.

Suddenly, I knew what I had to do. And it wasn't going to be easy. "During tryouts," I told Skip, "I made someone look bad so that I'd look good. I feel lousy. It's affecting my game."

Skip tapped his fingers on the desk. I couldn't read the expression on his face. "This person's name is —?"

"Jason Webster."

"Ah, yes … I remember. Jason was trying out for right wing also. You boys were at the same level. I would have had a hard time choosing one over the other."

I swallowed hard. "Guess you picked the wrong guy." My eyes started to fill. My breath came out in spurts.

"Hey, take it easy," Skip said.

"He was my friend," I explained. A couple of tears trickled down my cheek. I tried to mop them up with my sleeve.

"Don't worry about a little water," Skip said, nudging a box of Kleenex my way.

Pulling my Wave jersey out of my bag, I put it on the desk. "Can I go now?"

"I'm not finished," Skip said. "There is something you should know. Before the second tryout, Jason came to me and explained that he had enrolled in art classes every Tuesday. If he made the team, he would miss one practice a week. We need a full commitment at this level. That is the reason why I chose you over him."

"You mean …"

He nodded. "And by the way, I did see you hook Jason, and I was not impressed. But I saw other qualities in you — including drive and enthusiasm. After today, I also know you have a conscience. And that's a good thing."

I wiped my face with my sleeve.

"You made the team on your own merit, son."

My head was swirling. "Does this mean I'm not cut?"

"What gave you that idea?" Skip asked.

"Doesn't matter," I said, jumping up. "I'm back!" I grabbed my jersey. "Thanks, Skip."

"Now about your performance …"

"Don't worry. I'll do better. I won't let you down. You'll see. See, ya, Scotty."

Scotty laughed and gave me a wave. I got up to leave, then remembered something and sat back down. "About Dillon," I said. "Deep down, he's a good guy, and he's our best defenceman. I think —"

Skip cut me off. "Dillon has the talent of a young Bobby Orr. He plays solid defence, and takes every opportunity to go on the offence. But Bobby Orr was a good sportsman, and I can't say the same for Dillon."

"But he loves hockey," I insisted. "He can change."

Skip clasped his hands together and looked directly in my eyes. "Dillon is reckless on the ice. His actions put other players in danger. Believe me, Matt, I didn't come to this decision lightly. Letting a player go is the hardest part of a coach's job. But ultimately I am responsible for the team."

"I know he screwed up," I said. "Give him another chance."

"Dillon's not ready for a second chance," Skip said. "He has to earn the right to play."

"But …"

Skip raised a hand to silence me. "Bad hits have taken too many players out of the game. I know first-hand how it feels. Years ago, I thought I had a bright hockey future. My dream got destroyed when some goon hooked his stick around my knee and checked me into the boards. That check tore the ligaments

right off the bone. I never could play the same after."
Skip winced at the memory.

I realized he was not going to change his mind about Dillon.

17 Back in the Game

Jason was away when I looked for him at school the next day. Turns out, he had come down with strep throat. Our showdown would have to wait.

Dillon was also away. After getting kicked off the team — who could blame him?

On Saturday I headed over to Dillon's to see how he was doing. No one answered the door, and the car was missing. For days following our game, things were quiet in Lakeside.

Mrs. Carson was marking papers when I walked up to her desk.

"Excuse me," I said, "where's Dillon?"

"Away," she said.

"Where'd he go?" I insisted.

"That's confidential information," she said, keeping her eyes trained on the paper in front of her.

Amy tapped me on the shoulder. "He's gone to Toronto."

"Are you sure?"

"Yep, I overheard her telling the cashier at the bank. She was withdrawing a lot of money."

Toronto. Wow! His plan worked. He had caused so much trouble in Lakeside that his parents gave in and moved back. I was impressed for about five seconds. Then it hit me: He left without saying goodbye. He was back with his real friends —Spider and that other kid. Go figure, I had actually thought he liked me.

Forget him. I had other things on my mind. Jason was back at school, so at recess, I cornered him and Chen by the water fountain.

"Nice going, Jayce!" I called, jogging up behind them. "Blaming me when you didn't make the team."

Chen shot Jason a look. "I thought you were going to tell him."

Jason grinned sheepishly. "I wanted him to suffer first." He turned and spoke directly to me. "But then you started hanging out with Dillon. After a while, I figured it didn't matter."

"Didn't matter! Because of you, I psyched myself out of the game. I could hardly play."

"Yeah, well, I haven't forgotten what you did."

Chen stepped in. "Hey guys, this has gone on too long. You both messed up. Just forget it."

Deep down, I wanted things to be normal again. I hesitated, then cautiously said, "Maybe."

Jason thought for a moment. "Come on," he said, hitting my shoulder. "Let's play soccer."

Slowly, everything fell back into place. Chen and Jason were my buds — at least we were getting there; Kassy was just a friend; and Dillon lived in Toronto. My life had gone in a complete circle.

On Saturday, though, as I left the mall, I was taken aback to see a familiar-looking car buzz by. A thought occurred to me. When I got home, I jumped on my bike and rode over to Dillon's house. A man answered the door. He was tall, his head barely clearing the doorframe. He wore a dark, closely trimmed beard.

"Oh," I said, turning to leave. "I was looking for Dillon. We played hockey together."

"Your name is —?"

"Matt Gander."

The door swung open. "Come in!" the man boomed, greeting me like an old friend. "I'm Dillon's father."

"You are?" I stood there, gawking up like an idiot. Dillon's dad had never seemed real before. The man had consisted of angry words in brief clips of conversation.

"Dillon will be happy to see you," he said, ushering me upstairs.

I stopped on the second step and turned. "I thought he moved back to Toronto."

"Now where'd you get an idea like that?"

Mr. McPhail said, scratching his beard. "We think Lakeside is a terrific town."

"B-but," I stammered. "The house — no one answered. And my friend said Dillon had gone to Toronto."

"Dillon and his mom came down for a few days to help me pack my apartment," he explained. "I've moved to Lakeside for good, but I haven't even found a job yet." For some reason that made him smile. "We'll make it work," he said. "The important thing is that I spend time with my family. Plus," he added, wiping his brow, "No more highway traffic."

Dillon had been kicked off the hockey team, and now he was stuck living in Lakeside permanently. He was going to be in one scary mood. I knocked on his bedroom door.

"Come in!" Jason called.

What the —? Those two didn't hang out together! When I entered, I found Jason and Dillon sprawled out on the carpet, gripping charcoal pencils. Sketchpads lay on the floor in front of them.

I sat on the edge of Dillon's bed, not knowing what to say. So much had gone down lately. "Your dad told me you're stuck here for good," I fumbled out. "Too bad."

"Not really," Dillon said, sitting up. "When I got back to Toronto, things weren't the same with my old friends. We hardly talked. Besides, Lakeside's grown on me. Weird, eh? All along, I was determined to stick it to my parents for making me move, but I ended up sticking it to myself."

"Yeah," I agreed. "You did some damage."

I turned to Jason. "What are you doing here?"

He held up his sketchpad. "Showing Dillon some shading techniques."

"Seriously," I said, laughing.

"He missed the first two classes. I'm helping him catch up."

Dillon saw the look of disbelief on my face. "My counsellor suggested I take art classes, because I like to draw. He said I should take my anger out on paper instead of at the hockey rink."

"You're listening to the counsellor?" I was impressed, but this didn't sound like Dillon.

"It's not like you think," he said. "The counsellor's on my side. He's helping me to work out a plan — one that will get me back into hockey. By this time next year, I'll be playing Triple A again."

"But, your parents. I thought …"

"Now that my dad's living here, my parents will be able to take me to tournaments," Dillon said. "All I have to do is stop messing up."

I gave him a dubious look.

He laughed. "It's not so hard when you want something bad enough."

"Hockey?"

"What else?"

Grabbing a football from his shelf, I fired it at him, just kidding around. He didn't laugh when it hit his leg.

"Ow!" He grabbed his leg protectively.

"Oops, sorry," I said, shrugging. "Still bad, eh?"

"Getting better," he said. "My mom almost fainted when I finally showed her. She sent me straight to the hospital. A surgeon cut my leg open to drain the infection. Now the doctor says no sports until it heals. So, in a weird way, things worked out. I couldn't play hockey anyway."

I sat back amazed. "So, like, it's all good!"

"I'm working on it." He tossed his pencil on the floor. "Hey, you want to get something from the kitchen? We need a break from drawing."

"Uh … I can't. I've got a practice in an hour."

"On Saturday? It's not on the schedule."

"A game got cancelled," I explained. "Skip scooped up the ice time. He wants to break in the new defenceman before the next game."

"He'll never replace me," Dillon said, as I headed out the door.

That's for sure, I thought. In more ways than one.

Dad dropped me off at the Shoreline Arena during his break at the department store. After I got dressed, I stood by the gate, waiting for the practice to begin. Trent Sowinski walked up to me.

"How's your head?" I asked.

"Getting better," he said, rapping his knuckles on his forehead. "Ask me a question. Any question."

"What's five plus twelve?"

"Duh ..." He stared up in the air. "I dunno."

The guy cracked me up. "What are you doing here?" I asked.

"Looking out for my little cousin. Skip brought her up from the A/E team to play defence."

"Did you say *her*?"

"Yeah, her name's Leah."

"Defence?" I laughed. "A girl?"

"She's good," Trent said. "You'll see. Here she comes."

A girl approached, holding her helmet. Her long, brown hair was pulled back in a ponytail.

"She's not very big," I observed.

"I'm bigger than you are," she said, proving it, by standing next to me. "Besides, Trent's been working with me. Technique is more important than big muscles."

I stepped back. "Awesome!" I said. "Skip wouldn't have picked you if you weren't good enough. I was surprised. That's all."

"Actually, I am kind of nervous," she admitted. "I've never played at the 'A' level. Hope I'm okay."

I knew how she felt. Believing in yourself is hard at times. I also knew it was something she'd have to prove to herself.

Belch came up behind us. "Hey, Leah!" he said, with a corny smile. "How's it going?"

"We go to the same school," he explained to me. The four of us stood there talking for a few minutes. Something seemed different about Belch. He didn't burp around Leah. The poor guy — girls had gotten to him already.

The Zamboni took a few more laps, then sped out the exit. Belch skated off with Leah to practice some defensive moves.

I skated a few laps. My legs felt strong. My skates found a new speed. I wound up at the blue line, took a slapshot on the empty net and scored.